HOPE
ABANDONED

J.K. HOOKE

MILTON & HUGO L.L.C.
4407 Park Ave., Suite 5
Union City, NJ 07087, USA

Website: *www. miltonandhugo.com*
Hotline: *1- 888-778-0033*
Email: *info@miltonandhugo.com*

Ordering Information:
Quantity sales. Special discounts are granted to corporations, associations, and other organizations. For more information on these discounts, please reach out to the publisher using the contact information provided above.

Library of Congress Control Number: 2024920490
ISBN-13:   979-8-89285-325-5   [Paperback Edition]
                    979-8-89285-326-2   [Hardback Edition]
                    979-8-89285-324-8   [Digital Edition]

Rev. date: 09/18/2024

CONTENTS

PROLOGUE

In a timeless void

Life sucks! As if the world personally went out of her way to place a curse on me. But what can you expect from a divine being that's *literally* a dog.

Hell!!! In the first war, I lost my love, my chance at happiness, my friends and then the village I had come to call home ostracized me. But then, for a moment that seemed to last like the blink of an eye... there was peace.

Yet even that went to hell, the quiet life I was seeking, GONE!

Everything I worked on blew up —*literally*— in my face. Then, once again I got dragged into a supernatural war just to be used by God himself for the second time. Lost a lot of friends, got attacked by my ex-lover who I thought was DEAD!!!

Things did start to look up... that is until the massive battle with the Archangel Michael.

That was two years ago.

"You know!!! You read the first book about our hell, now I hope you can learn from the continuation of our story, for everything is not as it seems and as I stated in the beginning, they're all still dead."

June 15th, 2022

At the request of Roving Angel, Dehaas—High Leader of the Angels and Acting Head of Heaven—to meet with a rogue angelic leader who claimed to want peace with the beings of earth and, putting an end to the senseless violence. Naturally we agreed that should this leader's intentions be sincere, then we would hold a peace treaty in the tree of elders.

The mission itself was purely routine. Scout, Observe, Greet or *SOG* for short. There was no need for an assassination, but there is a reason the request was so secretive. When the parchment arrived everyone except for Dehaas, myself, and Steefas were asked to vacate the room before the mission details were disclosed. In the past, Ailani would have been one of the members to stay with us, as my prodigy and Second in command. However, that was before she lost her memories during the war with Michael. Now though, she is a simple house wife with a child on the way.

It was during this briefing that we then learned the name of the Angel. He went by the name of Gurdímark, leader of the Cobrînaux Faction comprising approximately forty to fifty Angels. Being so small, they tended to keep to themselves and away from any of the larger conflicts that have really died down to skirmishes.

This faction also does well to act as eyes and ears for both sides though. It was a strange arrangement, yet I guess they got tired of the pointless squabbles amongst the divided angels that would often chase away their subordinates. This would be a good chance to have one less enemy to fight in the long run. As the saying goes…

"You can only remain neutral for so long before you're forced back into conflict by outside interference."

The meeting itself was uneventful. Held in a dark cavern that was cool and damp. The perfect location to avoid prying eyes and easy to escape from anyone of the numerous passageways that littered the sides of the cavern. Holding a civil conversation which ended with an agreement to meet with a few other Angelic leaders of their own respective factions. This time, it would include the leaders of our current council. Mind you, we would not just take the word of the angels at heart. We of course had our suspicions that they would attempt an ambush to slaughter the lords from our council. To counteract this, I will keep Hägrīs, Arkain, Dehaas and Aarönin in a different tree entirely. Awaiting the signal that everything was safe. Should things go awry, then we were to reconvene at my house.

Over two years and with the help of the villagers, Steefas, and his children I hollowed out the foundations of my tree without killing it or ruining the structural integrity. Thus creating the anti-angelic- demonic bunker with a labyrinth of tunnels running under the forest of Véchenti at least five hundred feet under the surface. It was a huge city.

IN A TIMELESS VOID

A divine being observed through an orb of liquid mercury watching a young woman talk to an atrium full of God's creations. **"Two years after the war between Angels and other creatures began. Two years since life was forced to choose sides again, we would never have guessed that our enemy would be the Angels this go around."** The woman in her twenties began.

"First; Cain—stubborn bastard that he was— gave his left arm and right leg for us, so we would make it out of the enemy's encampment where we had been ambushed by a couple of shapeshifters." The young woman said to the populated atrium. A brazier alight, causing shadows to flicker in the night. The distant sound of a building crumbling as it turned into rubble from age.

"**Next was my mother, Ailani, who lost her memory a little over a year ago and thought that Janix was just a family friend.**" Those who were there when their friends bowed their heads. As they remembered the many other allies and friends who were lost or captured in this long war... The woman in question was there for most of it, there for the rising of *Hell bringer*, and there for the loss of so many friends.

However, in the woman's story, she continued as from the point where they all waited for the peace talks to begin, primarily waiting for the angels who had yet to arrive. "**I'm going to tell you about the greatest heroes that lived before the end times, before the *Darkness* that overtook most of the known world.**" The woman finished with a humbled tone. "**I'm going to tell you the story about my family.**"

CHAPTER 1

Surprise Attack

June 19th, 2022

Now

The day started warm and humid. Cooled with a gentle breeze that rustled the leaves and adding a calming effect. Yet what would normally be a beautiful and tranquil day, was ruined by heavy animosity at the severity and importance of today. You see, today is the day of the negotiations between some smaller factions of angels, thus another step closer to the end of war.

Yet for me it didn't feel like the end, after being forced into yet another war which should have never begun in the first place. Another war that caused pain and sadness to so many. Remembering the events that brought me back just brought a bitter taste to my mouth as I couldn't help but be plagued by thoughts. Observing the room, I took note of every little detail that there was.

In the Tree of Elders was a large room, rows of tables divided on both sides resembling that of a courtroom or mess hall. A primary podium in the front fashioned out of solid Iron wood laced with golden trim giving an extravagant and formal look. In the very back of the room, separated by a four foot tall oak fence guard, was a convening area where all could talk and meet during waiting periods.

This is where myself, Alex, his pregnant wife; Ailani, their bodyguards; Thomas and Ashlee as well Flores who stood off to the side drinking a pint of mead. All of us weary from two years of fighting; a costly two years. But, a few nights ago I was on a mission that led us to this moment.

The people here now are Generals of various factions for humans. Alex who ranked up to becoming the General of our foot soldiers, Flores took over Ailani's position as General of the Archers, Thomas and Ashlee were the heads of a small mercenary division that are utilized as contingents for explosive and guerrilla warfare. Everyone had a role to play, and a place at this table, as for myself, much to my own dismay was appointed High Commander as well as village councilor. Leader to the United Forces of Véchenti.

Everyone was entertaining themselves with talk of old missions and future plans to come. That is, until it was interrupted by a very distinct

CLIP, THUD, CLOP, THUD

All eyes turned to the door where a scarred old man came clopping in with his peg-leg and missing left arm. He didn't look like much in his very disheveled appearance. Large belly from years of drinking and eating without a care in the world, his left sleeve dangling loose from his missing limb, the wooden peg leg creating a rhythmic beat as he walked.

Silence filled the room as all eyes fell on Cain as he limped in with confidence. Turning his burned and scarred head towards our little group, he acknowledged myself and Flores with a nod before turning to the couple, "Ailani, Alex, how's the little one doing?" He asked. It was a simple question that irritatingly still saddened me as I stood with Flores, pouring myself a pint.

"Oh Cain, the baby is doing fine, I'm sure it'll be a strong boy just like his father." Ailani said before looking at Alex with love and kissing him on the cheek. Looking away as Alex began exclaiming that it could be a beautiful girl like her mother, I went back to my conversation with Flores who humored me with a pleasant change of subject. It wasn't the best solution, but it's better than the alternative of drinking myself under a table.

Who'd have thought that Alex who Ailani initially hated would suddenly become that source of growing and maturing that he needed. As long as he treats her well— Which Steefas threatened Alex once he found out what happened to her memories— I won't have a problem residing in the shadows of their happy family.

I was listening to Flores babble about the happenings of work and how his archer battalions have been working on new arrows and implementing them into various tactics. He also talked about the girl he was talking to and hoping to ask out should the timing prove convenient. In the middle of Flores rambling, I allowed my mind to branch and extend to my faithful friend and closest thing I had to a brother who was sitting by the doorway.

'*Steefas, sometimes I wish that I would just die...*' It wasn't the first time I'd made the comment. Yet, Steefas, King of the Hellhounds, Lord of Shadows and Fire, understood what I meant. Replying with a wolfish chuckle.

'*Now, now Master, you and I both know that if you were to die, then one; I'd have to raze most of the area until I got revenge for you or died myself. Don't think that my children don't share the same sentiments too, you did spoil most of them after all.*' Steefas turned his wolf head towards me, the glowing red gleam in his eye was a simplistic way of telling me that although he said it in jest, he was also deadly serious about the statement he made.

'*Most importantly, your old mate, though she doesn't remember you, would still be distraught.*'

3

'I know, I know... why don't you go outside and help your son keep watch?' I glanced up from my pint to see Steefas was already fading into a shadow. Damn that demonic wolf.

As Flores finished his slight rambling, I looked at him asking, "Flores, how long has it been since we were supposed to start?" He looked at his gift from the Djinn community, a magnificent little time keeping device called *Watch*. It's a golden case and little gears with a glass film over the top as well as two little arrows fixed in the center that somehow moved every hour. This allowed us to synchronize our movements and plan well timed attacks. Only the highest leaders had one... except for Flores of course as he was getting pretty friendly with a feminine Djinn who seems to have taken a fancy to him.

"We should have started this meeting ten mikes ago." Frowning, I couldn't shake the feeling that something's off. I looked at everyone while thumbing the hilts of my throwing knives, securely tucked and hidden into my belt line.

Something is seriously wrong. Today's meeting was supposed to negotiate the peace between the angels and beings of Vèrchenti forest. However, the angels are already late.

'LOOK OUT!!!'

Steefas screamed at me telepathically followed by a large ballistae imbedding itself inches from my face. It had a mark that made my blood boil in anger.

"GET DOWN!!!" Cain screamed as he tackled Alex to keep themselves down. A flaming rock crashed through the ceiling crushing Alex two bodyguards. They were crushed instantly on impact and turned into nothing more than smoldering limbs and gore. Alex was the first to recover, "THE HELL WAS THAT!?!!" He exclaimed.

'Steefas, SITREP.' I ordered telepathically while coming up with our plan of action.

'Three hundred meters due east and closing, a small faction of Angels, plus a few Djinn's controlling Catapults and Ballistae farther back. I don't know how they got the weapons through without anyone seeing. We will buy you some time but y'all have to get out of here!'

"DAMN IT!" I relayed the situation report to our group while telling Steefas to do his best, Steefas would meet up later when we got away safely. I drew one of my knives and prepared for a fight. Knives are absolutely not my preferred weapon yet they are all I have at this moment.

"CAIN, ALEX! GET EVERYONE OUT OF HERE!" I ordered as another flaming stone came in from the wall knocking a pile of stones and roofing onto Flores who was now trapped. Ailani was screaming in fear and attempting to help Alex who was wounded from shrapnel of a stone.

In an instant, the room was filled with angelic light. Signaling a divine one had just appeared. When it evaporated Dehaas and Andreas were there cutting open a swirling black portal before grabbing me.

"Get the girl out of here, secure a location, fix her memories. Her priestess powers will be needed again." I didn't have time to question him so I tried to get Steefas a location to meet.

'Steefas, meeting location Zulax...' that was all I was able to relay before another stone impacted the house and a sharp pain erupted in my chest. Dehaas chucked me and Ailani through the vortex which instantly deposited us to our new location. My head hit something solid once we exited the portal before I blacked out completely.

HOURS LATER

Pain... I woke up to pain in the left side of my chest and beams of light hitting my face. As we were tossed, I guess I'd taken shrapnel from a stone which was still sticking out of my chest in a sickening manner.

With a grunt of effort, I ripped the stone from my body, spilling several lines of blood before it slowed to a slight leak. It was moments like this that I was thankful for being a hybrid. Then I moved to help Ailani who was a few meters from me. She was fine, if not a little disheveled. Reaching out with spiritual energy, I also identified that her and Alex's child was just fine. The unborn's heart is still strong as ever.

As for myself, my wound was already healing but Ailani wouldn't understand as we never discussed the extent of my powers with her when Alex and I would meet. So I cleaned and wrapped the wound before finally stopping to observe the area. Taking notice of the canopy above us. It seemed that the forest was… peaceful if not extremely humid. Sitting here I could feel my body perspiring, my throat dry and lips chapped. There seemed to be no-one around us, not even the sign of a village. Nothing but the forest and a tall mountain peak that I could make out in the distance through the foliage. Taking notice that Ailani was still unconscious, I allowed my wings to extend. Flying high into the clouds getting a layout of the land. Well, I attempted anyway as I learned from my flight… I still had no idea where the hell we were.

'Steefas?'

…

'Steefas you there?'

…

Great…

From the sky though, I could make out a winding river cutting through the forest until disappearing under the canopy. The placement of the sun and mountain range to my back, made me guess we'd been dropped somewhere west of Mt. Sīusęn. This is going to be a problem as there is no way to get over or around it. Mt. Sīusęn is an Iron mountain that is mined for its ore; however, the men mining it have only ever made it about 25 feet into the mountain itself. Sadly, this meant that the idea of finding a tunnel through the belly of said mountain was slim to none. Given that the mountain is over fifteen thousand feet high, there is no way in hell I'd be able to fly over it with a pregnant Ailani. That said, going around would be too long...

"Damn it!" I exclaimed.

Out of everything, one thing was certain. When Ailani woke up, we had to get moving to meet up with Steefas and the other lords. I had to have faith my Generals were competent enough to make it to safety on their own. Until then, I allowed her to sleep while going out to forage and hunt. Catching small rabbits, I cooked them and flavored them with a few berries that I found. I've never traveled this far personally but I'd heard stories about places like this from Smee and Albright while they were on business travels. This type of area was always full of evil and bandits from what the merchants told me. We will have to be vigilant and cautious if we are to avoid trouble.

CHAPTER 2

Beginnings of an End

It wasn't until after a few hours that Ailani finally awoke from her slumber. Startled and confused that I was stoking a fire while keeping a cooked rabbit warm, I handed her the critter. Freshly cooked and began explaining the situation we were in. Thankfully, she took the explanation extremely well and agreed that after she ate, we would make some movements before the end of the day.

Laughing to myself, I should have known better. Even without her memories, she's the tenacious survivor that I trained her to be. That said, I still need to be conscious of the child within her womb, though it may not be mine, I would not let anything happen to hers or Alex's offspring. I'd never be able to look her in the eyes again if anything happened.

AN HOUR LATER

"You know Janix," She began as I helped her down from a ledge. "I do believe that this is the most time we've ever been around each other since the final battle." She said laughing with mirth... until she saw the pained expression that I tried and failed to hide. "Im... sorry?" She then replied confused.

"No, I'm the one that's sorry, Ailani." I said while pausing a moment before smirking, "You're right though, I'm usually on missions and taking care of matters in the village. Plus I train

Aarönin's children." Putting on my best fake smile; though, even I could tell it wasn't convincing. We continued in relative silence.

She was surprisingly quick, for a pregnant woman, able to keep a good pace allowing us to travel a greater distance than I thought we would have. Hell, it even got to the point that I was starting to think that maybe we should just fly out of here, at least I could still carry her a good distance so as to mitigate the amount of walking we had to do. That is… until Ailani noticed a trail of blood I was leaving when my makeshift bandage traversed from the wound, it wasn't a problem, it would be healed within the next hour or so. I adjusted the bandage before I kept us moving, letting her know that it was fine and we needed to reach our primary location for the day in order for us to meet up with Steefas by the end of the week.

She wouldn't leave it alone.

"Janix please! Just let me at least look at your wound." Ailani begged for the fifth time tonight.

"DAMN IT AILANI, I SAID I'M FINE!" I snapped at her while observing the area around me. I realized my mistake too late, looking at her and seeing tears in her eyes coupled with a look of confusion? I couldn't help but feel sorrow for her.

Damn it! I screamed at my own negligence of the situation, I had forgotten that Ailani had no memory of how I would heal. Nor any knowledge of her own divine prowess, we haven't been around each other often enough since she lost her memories. Then to save some strife, Alex doesn't bring me up much either —by my request— adding to the question *Who am I to her and her family.* In reality, I've become all but an enigma to her. Just a shadow that comes and goes in the night.

"Shit," I whispered under my breath, "Ailani" I began sighing. "I'm sorry, it's just, you really don't need to worry about me." I guess now was a good time as ever to start easing her back into it. Stopping by a large tree that was tall and well spread. It covered a wide area, giving us cover from any prying eyes in the sky. I took off my shirt and jacket exposing my scared torso to her for the first time--again-- and undressed the wound to show her. It wasn't a large wound anymore, hell, it was even healing fast enough that we could watch it.

It was the same as the first time she witnessed my quick healing, first was the initial shock and gasp, then the awe. Finally, she broke the silence.

"Janix… how is that even possible?" Pulling my shirt back on, I approached a rather large tree root, taking a moment to observe the area before addressing her.

"We're far enough for now," I said, laying my coat on the tree root. "Sit, this area is secure enough, and we have much to talk about." She complied before wrapping herself in the coat, it was quite clear that she enjoyed the softness of my white fur coat, made of a demonic sabertoothed arctic cat. Gifted to me by Steefas a few months ago after a *very* dramatic battle between them.

"Tell me Ailani, what's the last thing you remember before waking up during the battle two years ago?"

"I was working as a nurse, helping those on the battlefield." Sighing, I just continued.

"And what about Alex, me and the others?"

"I met Flores at the base on the same day I got there as the Doctor gave us the tour. Alex joined us the same day" she stopped before letting out a light chuckle to which I looked at here slightly bewildered. "Alex tried to help me learn how to fight, even if it was just to defend myself. I wasn't the greatest pupil…" she finished with a laugh to which I discreetly rolled my eyes—not the best? I mean if you count the near death sparring matches we held every other day on top of being personally trained by me. Not to mention the amount of scars I have from her damn saber.— She suddenly brought her hand to her head as if she were struck. Her expression was one of discomfort.

Raising my eyebrow, "You OK?" She looked confused for a moment before taking her hand away from her head, looking at me again.

"I'm... I'm fine" she responded, it was clear she was still a little miffed about something. "I don't remember much about how we left the base or how we made it to the village of Vèrchenti, Alex asked me to marry him one night under the moonlight..."

'So, this is the shell of my beloved?' I directed towards God. I never got an answer, no surprise.

"Overcome with emotion, I didn't even have the words to say yes right away, we got married the next day so there would be nothing stopping us from being happy at the end of this war. We then banded together, against the threats of the renegade Angels in which he was supposed to take Michaels place." I was listening intently, it would appear that her entire perspective of the eight months that we knew each other, had been altered and changed to that of Alex. "It was after three days of marching that we assaulted the mountain, so many people... so many deaths in that fight, Janix..." I just hung my head in honor of those that we lost. Once again, she clutched her head as if it hurt her to even think about what she was saying. Getting up to try and help her, time suddenly froze, the light from the fire still kept the area lit as some of the shadows tried to overtake us.

"You must let her complete the journey," Andreas voiced from behind me before manifesting out of the shadows, "only once the visions are over can she truly heal and stop feeling pain."

"And what is the purpose? Why must I force her to remember such horrid memories?" It didn't make any sense to me, we've been doing fine, the team, me and the rest of the warriors at Vèrchenti had everything under control.

"A new evil is encroaching this world, even my father is shutting himself off from the rest of the world and instead of torturing the damned, he's arming them which hasn't been done in two millennium. This is all I can tell you for now," Andreas was already fading into the shadows, "but you must make it to the base of the mountain, I will tell you more then." He was gone, and time resumed again.

Ailani looked up at me and gave me a simple nod that she was fine.

"Alex was fighting with all he had, rallying the warriors together and pushing us forward. As the wounded came back I treated them but..." pausing, her breath caught for a moment like she had to think, "I heard that Alex had been struck down, so I ran out to the battlefield looking for him which is when I saw you." She looked at me smiling, "I never did thank you for saving us did I?" This caught my attention, as her memories block me out all the way to the battle that nearly ended our days. "Janix." she began, "Aarönin's children always ask me the strangest things, like if I'll ever fight again. Its like they know me as a different person compared to that of my healing profession. You wouldn't know why would you?" She asked with a very perplexed look. I could only give her a small look before drawing my blades, an obsidian saber, beautiful and deadly. The other, a breathtaking machete that appeared alive like a swirl of galaxies compressed into the form of a blade, a machete of Matter, I thought for a moment, looking at the blades as did Ailani. She was transfixed by the look of her old saber, and even seemed like she wanted to reach out to take it.

My mind trailed again, Ailani, she used to be an incredible priestess and general. Master with her Saber and Bow, whose powers were beyond that of other mortal's, a holy servant. One might even say she was becoming a powerful sorceress. Not only this, but she was also my best friend and girlfriend... Yet, even the lord can't stop fate from forging its cruel path.

"The history of these blades, though new, is a very sad one. This saber was a gift to the girl I loved once," Ailani listened intently, extremely interested and wanted to know more than the little bit that she was always told about me... which was virtually nothing. "Fate then found it fitting to take her away." I paused before taking a breath. I began a small dance of expert movements with the blades. "When she was taken from me," my body flowed with the blades like water, passing through the air. "I picked it up and kept it safe for the day that I may need it," every move I made was sharp, precise, and deadly "or find the right person to pass it on too." Ailani, though interested, was no doubt wondering why I was telling her a story about our blades and not myself.

"You don't remember, but we knew each other before that battle..." I continued ending my dance of blades, which she just smiled at. "What if I told you that you were more than that of a medical worker." This time she looked confused but even more interested. "More than Alex's wife, more than everything you remember."

Sheathing my Machete, I held the obsidian saber which I had gifted her so long ago now.

"This blade is made of the hardest materials known to the world, blessed in the temples of the north by a powerful priestess, sharpest blade ever created... aside from my machete of course." I finished that last part with a chuckle before using it to slice a tree down which had a base of five inches. She still had her eyes locked on the deadly blade, transfixed by its beauty. Placing my right hand on the center of the blunt edge, and my left holding the ricasso, I offered her the grip.

Slowly, she allowed herself to wrap her fingers around the grip. "You weren't just medical help Ailani, you were a General, one of the greatest fighters to ever live, second to none but myself and the greatest student I've ever trained." This was the truth, even now, I can see my teaching instilled in her. It showed in the way she held the Saber Standing tall, I looked upon her as I recited her titles which she earned and worked so hard for.

"Commander of the Archer battalion, High priestess to the Order of Adonai, Healer of Legions, Sorceress and Cheater of **Death**."

There was silence as I finished reciting her titles. She stared at me. Positively dumbfounded by what I told her. It seemed as if she was deep in thought, giving me hope, to why she's so important, and her role. And why we were the ones on the run.

CHAPTER 3

Disappearance and Storms

Ailani finally spoke up laughing. "Oh stop it Janix, you and I both know I couldn't hurt a fly. You jest too much." She said, clutching her stomach. I could only sigh, wishing I didn't have to help her find out this way.

"Then it should be easy," I said resting my right hand on the pommel of my machete before wrapping my fingers around the leather grip, "for me to kill you!" I finished with a hard gaze drawing my machete.

"What are y…?" That was as far as she got when I lashed out with a basic but fast slash at her head. Quick as lightning, she diverted the blade away and got into a fighting stance. Not bad for a pregnant woman.

"Then how were you able to block one of my attacks," I asked before faking and going for her arm this time. Just as quick, she parried before attacking with one of her own slashes and jabs. Quick and precise, just as I taught her.

"You may not remember," I said, locking eyes with her, remembering all the fun duels we used to have. "But my training doesn't leave the body so easily." I finished as our blades locked and this time I felt the cool blade puncture my skin as she tilted hers in such a way that it entered my arm.

"JANIX, WHAT ARE YOU DOING!" She screamed, eyes flashing silver making me reel. Too late I realized what was about to happen as my eyes widened in surprise. A pulse of energy was sent at me, hitting me square in the chest and throwing me back into a tree, crushing the bark and toppling it. Her eyes widened, comprehending what just happened. Ailani, stood there in shock, watching as I stood with a grunt of effort. We both took in the tree that was toppled from her outburst, even after all this time, she still packs a punch.

I couldn't help but laugh. A good hearty and drunk laugh.

"Now do you understand what I'm telling you?" I asked walking up while sheathing my machete.

"Janix... how did I..." she doubled over, dropping her saber and clutching her head in pain. My mirth fell as I ran over to her.

"Don't fight them Ailani, what you're experiencing are memories long suppressed. They are reemerging to the front of your mind's consciousness." I didn't like it, but she needed to see these visions. Whatever they were, would help her get through this, and from what the Roving Angels said, they could be the only reason that she survives.

I knelt to the side, ready to react if anything bad started to happen. Agonizingly, I watched as her eyes rolled into the back of her head, a bluish-violet aura flowed around her. It was as if a dam had broken in her mind, she started thrashing on the ground as wind began to pick up. The moon above the tree line seemed to brighten as this was happening and from a distance, the howls of feral wolves could be heard. Her veins began to turn black as it seemed that more power was getting charged. Orbs of spiritual energy began flowing into her. I don't know what magic is at work right now, but it's old and malicious. But then, there was silence.

Ailani stopped thrashing allowing her eyes to shut momentarily before opening emitting a blue light from her eyes followed by the release a feral scream so loud and powerful a shockwave resounded through the area blasting through the land. The wind around us whipped and turned into a swirling vortex with us in the center of its eye. Her screams intensified while the raging storm got more powerful. Coupled with that of loud thunder and harsh lighting until a large bolt struck her. My ears rung from the blast as more struck all around me. I was blown back again when a bolt hit me in the chest, smoke rose creating a screen that blocked out everything in front of me.

"Ailani?" I asked before trying to crawl to where she was. Somethings wrong, her aura wasn't there… it wasn't even in the area. "Ailani?" I asked as my eyes cleared. Where she had been laying, was nothing. Literally nothing but an imprint in the earth where she had been laying just seconds before and untouched by the flames. Panic set in as I realized something had to have happened.

"AILANI WHERE ARE YOU?" My wings fully extended and with a mighty flap, I was soaring in the air looking for her.

No! I thought flying over the forest

No! No! I repeated while looking, fear setting into me.

No! No! No!

"AILANI!!!" I yelled, screaming into the night. My mixed blood caused Angelic and Demonic energy to pulse before creating a decimating shockwave one hundred meters around me uprooting trees and destroying large portions of forest while setting surrounding trees ablaze. She's nowhere near me… Where the hell did Ailani go…

The sky rumbled as black lightning flashed all around me. It was as if I were a conductor of sorts, just barely dodging as lightning struck too close for comfort. The only reason I wasn't dead yet was thanks to my years of experience, and a lot of luck as I was barely missing the hellish lighting.

That is… until I felt the buildup of electric pressure around me, this next blast of lightning would hit me and not even I could dodge it this time. From the way that these lightning bolts felt, the amount of energy they exerted meant one thing. Their composition was that of anti-matter, the complete opposite of my own blade. One strike is all it would take to kill me. It will literally tear me apart before= scattering my essence to the winds and cosmos.

Where the hell was this lightning coming from? Closing my eyes, a bright flash illuminated the land and air around me, so bright that even I waited for the shock that never came. Something solid slammed into me throwing me away from the energy and into the ground below. It was an odd landing though, something wet and squishy. The smell of sulfuric gas and burning hair was strong, on top of this nagging feeling in the back of my head.

Opening my eyes, I was greeted by the sight of a transformed Lycan. Slowly, I watched as his snout started to retract into his face and form back into that of a human appearance. His arms shortened, claws receding into his hands and dog-like legs reconfigured into human legs. Long locks of dusty brown hair fell over his face, he looked... sickly and thin, to the point that I could actually see most of his skeletal features.

"Glad *you're...* ok." He rasped before passing out from exertion.

Looking down on this malnourished Lycan only to see he was thin and covered in scars before his body started disintegrating into nothingness. From his mouth, black mist slowly exited before disappearing into the air. This lycan was already dead and had been possessed by one of Lucifer's followers. He had taken the hit of the lightning which confused me to where he'd come from.

The area itself appeared to be silent, nothing made a sound, even the wind stopped blowing, leaving the entire forest in an eerie silence. Something was wrong, my instincts going crazy as I drew my machete. Drums sounded deep within the forest, getting louder and faster, louder, louder, LOUDER, **LOUDER!!!!**

Looking around, the sound of the drums ceased, replaced by the sound of a bell. Loud and strong as if a meeting were being called in a village. But that was impossible, when I had

18

done my survey flight, there were no villages for miles. Only forest and the winding river that... disappeared under a large canopy of trees. Sheathing my machete, I took off through the forest at a dead sprint as questions riddled my mind.

How could I have missed it? Approaching the top of the trees I was about to break through the branches to what was hopefully the village that must have Ailani. Before I could though the ringing got louder and more urgent. Then nets from all around flew at me catching me by surprise. Yelling curses and getting more tangled, I was unable to redraw my machete. I wouldn't need a weapon due to my other worldly powers, but I figured that this may be the best way to locate Ailani. If she is in the home of these locals, then I need to get both of us out of here and continue moving to the base of the mountainside.

I ended up with a bag over my head and my takers began moving me somewhere. This wasn't a problem as I was carried, unceremoniously but still carried. I then felt the all too familiar feeling of cold steel being placed around my ankles and wrists to which I just chuckled at. This brought back memories of when I was imprisoned with Zoe and Lucas. With that thought in mind, my own mind began to trail off.

What am I to do when dealing with whoever these kidnappers were. I couldn't let them go free, not after this, but at the same time I felt no malicious intent and therefore figured that they were just taking appropriate action to an outsider intruding on their land. I'll cause a little havoc if need be and then we'll both be on our way. With any luck it'll be simple and easy. At least that's what I thought until I was unceremoniously dumped on the ground finding my mask coming off allowing me to see my environment again. It was then that I noticed I was in the presence of someone I thought I had left back in the old bunker. Before me, with cold calculating eyes and an angry expression was the older face much similar to that of the one I loved. Before me... was Ailani's sister... Katrina.

CHAPTER 4

Sister of My Love

Katrina sat on a throne made of two trees that intertwined together. To her left was a large dog that resembled that of a doberman, with long ears and sharp fangs bared at me, yet it had the body of a wild cat and the tail of a green pit viper. To her right was a beautiful sword that seemed to be made of diamond. The hilt, studded with blood rubies and the pommel topped with gold. It was a fancy looking blade to say the least.

Clearing her throat, I was brought back to her appearance which was no more friendly than this welcome. She wore black steel boots with spikes protruding at the base of her toes, jutting out just above her ankle in the opposite direction. Then just above her kneecaps, the metal extended with two more jutting back. Steel gauntlets with razor edges rode along her forearm, the blades glistening in the torch light. The rest of her body is covered by a skin tight dark leather suit with pointed steel shoulder pads, extending three inches away from her face. Upon her head was a crown of silver and obsidian. She reminded me so much of her younger sister.

"Katrina, it's been…"

"YOUR DARE TO SPEAK IN MY PRESENCE?" Her voice boomed, loud and proud. Full of apparent anger, though at what I don't know.

"Two and a half years ago, I watched you and my sister escape. Two and a half years ago, I had asked you to watch over her." Her tone was cold as ice, eyes sharp as daggers and piercing like that of a wicked saber. "Yet here you are now!" Spitting at me, "Before me, without my sister and the wings of mine enemies. WHAT SAY YOU! **ABOMINATION!**" I was grabbed by the neck and tossed at her feet by one of her supporters. Said supporter looked remarkably like Hägrīs, King of the Lycans.

I couldn't suppress the light hearted laughter that escaped my lips. This might not be as easy as I once thought it would be. Sighing, "Abomination am I?" Casting my gaze downward, remembering when Ailani had the same reaction to me and Steefas. "Your sister said something similar once, but we got over our differences—sort of, after Andreas intervened—and made it out alive. She was a true warrior, the greatest fighter that lived, second to only myself." I recited with pride, it was true after all. "But how about your soldier here? Why does he look like Hägrīs"

Katrina looked taken aback by my statement, "Was... So it's true then?" She said with tears in her eyes now before steeling her gaze. "She's dead... and you did nothing!" Seething this last part, she picked up her sword and held it to my throat. "Tell me why I shouldn't kill you where you lay?" Sighing, I reacted like lightning. Breaking my bonds and startling everyone in the room as I tipped the sword downwards with my right hand allowing it to barely miss my flesh, pushing off the ground with my left, I grabbed her wrist with my right. Pulling it to her throat and leaving all of us in a swift stalemate.

"Katrina, I don't want to hurt you, but I'm also not getting slain by you or your troops. Now please... order them to stand down!" I requested kindly; well, as kindly as one can while holding a potentially former ally hostage. Katrina cast an angry scowl at her subordinates. I understood she was trying to calculate her situation and running scenarios through her head. It seemed that she couldn't find a way out of this without either

her dying or a large number of her troops. So with a large sigh, she relaxed a little in my arms, snapped her fingers towards her guards who, simultaneously straightened up before sheathing their arms. Turning, they marched out of the room pulling the door with them. Once the large door shut with a loud thud, I released her arms and lightly pushed her away before she could get any ideas to attack me.

Taking a breath, "What are you doing on this side of the mountain, **monstrosity**!?" she spat. I couldn't help but roll my eyes at her stubbornness.

"If you will kindly allow me to explain. After the great battle between me and Michael, I assume you hadn't heard about it, but Ailani lost her memories." I paused, allowing her time to react and take in the information that she was obviously lacking. She held a stoic look, yet her eyes were a dead giveaway when they widened ever so slightly. When she didn't say anything, I continued, "She didn't remember anything, not us meeting, going to meet you or even about us saving the world from an angelic purge." My voice caught for just a second, all the emotions flooding back before I suppressed them again. "Her only memory was that of Alex and her group whom she'd arrived with. So... yes, she WAS the greatest. But also..." I paused looking at her with a light smile. "Congratulations, you're an Aunt to her and Alex's kid." Upon hearing this news, her eyes, which held that of being distraught, held pure rage.

"That pompous ingrate!" I saw her blue eyes flash dangerously, "Her memories were altered to that of being with that lewd sack of filth!" I flinched at her words, he was... an odd man at times, but he didn't deserve that.

"I admit, he is a unique man, but I promise you that he's not taken advantage of her," I began, eyebrows furrowed and a slight waver in my voice. All of our old memories flooding into my mind. "He's worked with her, matured with her, and they found love, real love in each other." A small smile graced my lips, I continued, "Not only did they help with the war effort, but they were able to marry and even begin the stages of… starting a family."

She seemed to be eyeing me heavily before asking her next question. "And how would you know if she's happy with him?"

We spent the better part of a half hour recounting the events that happened, from the days she met Alex and then just substituting Alex's name with what she and I had gone through. When I had finally finished the tale, she was sitting back on her throne, deep in thought and seemed to be at a loss of words.

"The way you talk about them, the way you talk about my sister… it makes me wonder if there was something between the two of you?" She asked with a look of intrigue and a raised eyebrow to which I just sighed. Turning away as I didn't trust my eyes to not give anything away,

"Perhaps there could have been. But it doesn't matter anymore. I am once again but a pawn to the Lord, one that wishes to rekindle the peace between mortal, Angel and beast." This was true, I loved Ailani enough to let her go… to go be with another man who brought her happiness. Another man who kept her out of danger and… then she was thrown with me, some protector I turned out to be…

"Where is my sister now? You said that both of you were at a meeting before getting chucked through a portal and ending up in my forest."

"I was instructed to help her remember, Andreas informed me that, for this new evil. It even has Lucifer cutting off hell and fortifying it. He's keeping to himself and dealing with a number of various complications." Looking up, I saw her waiting for me to finish.

"After I'd begun telling her about the past, this lightning storm gathered out of nowhere, she was reliving memories that I had hoped to keep from her mind. With a flash of light and black lightning striking our area, Ailani was gone. I had assumed that after I was captured by your group, that she was here. But now I know she isn't, and I must continue my search."

"No. you. will. not. *Janix*," a voice boomed all around the room. A crack opened up from the center of the stone floor and hands reached out of the earth. Fleshy skeletal hands pulling the bodies of eight misshapen warriors out of the ground and then behind them, Lucifer flew into the throne room. Landing in front of me with a gust of dust and wind, the room got colder. The torches barely keeping the shadows at bay, dimming and lowering to that of a small candle flame. Red light emanated from the crack before it faded and was gone. Lucifer stood with his eight warriors flanking each side of him. Each dawning pure white clothing, like that of high priests and a white mask over their heads with a goat symbol stitched into it. All of the priests, brandishing their own cutlass wrapped in a red and white cloth.

"*Sup Janix*" The lord of all that is evil greeted with a wave to which I sighed.

"What are you doing here Lucy?" We weren't friends, but during our missions, I'd have to deal with at least two demons which eventually lead up to us settling our differences... to a point. I no longer wanted to slaughter him on sight at least, and we had a mutual understanding to stay out of each other's way.

Smiling, he looked past me, "*Katrina, it's about time to introduce him to our mutual friends, I'm afraid that we don't have time to waste.*"

What was this... how do they know each other? How did Katrina get to this location, also how and where did she become queen? Finally, who are these friends that they spoke of.

"*Janix!*" Lucifer's voice broke me out of my stupor. "*Quit gawking and come with us.*"

"Where are we going? Who are we meeting?" I asked once he broke me out of my stupor. Smiling, he replied simply:

"*To meet the crafty one, the crafty owl.*"

CHAPTER 5

An Angry Owl

"The crafty what?" After living over a century, I pride myself for the fact that I've been humbled with the meeting of most living creatures known to man. So the fact that nothing came up in my memories involving an owl, not even legends completely baffled me.

"The Owl of Craftsmanship and Wisdom." Lucifer answered as we left the large throne room through two incredibly large iron doors that seemed to open inward into a dimly lit corridor which appeared to be never ending. Lucy's eight servants followed closely, as well as Katrina's warriors flanking us on the edges of the hallway. The shadows seemed to be trying to encroach on our little band. I couldn't help but notice an oddly familiar pair of eyes reflecting the light from a far corner but still hiding the owner.

"Janix, keep caution that although Rústicar is a calm being, he is unrefined and dislikes anyone touching his nicknacks." We stopped in front of large iron doors; doors that appeared to have been built for giants. In the center of both doors were large upside down Owl heads made of bronze. The eyes like that of yellow sapphires, it's expression wise, yet malicious. Their golden beaks were protruding outward and curved toward the ceiling. Flanking the door were large brasiers full of an odd looking liquid. My gut told me that they were full of blood though.

Lucifer cut his hand, allowing his angelic essence to flow out of him, and started chanting in a language that I couldn't understand. It was like the cross of angelic, demonic, and many other cultures, merged into one. It had its desired effect though, as black flames ignited before the flaming liquid drained onto a cupped shelf and traversed through crevices into the doors, illuminating the yellow sapphires. There was a series of clicking and mechanisms moving from within the door. The Owl heads, which appeared upside down began rotating until they were leering down at us with yellow light overlooking our group. Then with a final click, the doors opened inward letting us see a giant white owl. In a colossal nest that seemed to be made of books and metal devices, it sat in slumber. It's breathing, heard because of its vast size, caused a light breeze, its features resembled that of a great horned owl. However the body was slender and feathers puffed out. It was a magnificent creature, the likes of which I've never seen before.

However, as fast as the awe came to me, sorrow replaced it just as quickly... Ailani would have loved this. She's always had a thing for animals, and would've been ecstatic to meet one as puffy as this Owl. However, as cute as he looked, I knew that he held ancient knowledge. That he was on the level of being God-like, and even as powerful as I am, I held no doubt that he would end my existence with a simple spell.

DING, DING, DING.

"Rústīcar! Wake up you damn Owl, it's finally time that you met the one that's supposedly meant to end our suffering." Lucifer broadcasted it loudly, while I looked at him weird.

"What? Just cause I dress like a gentleman doesn't mean that I can't have a little fun..." As he finished, a large beak snapped at the place that he was just moments ago. Lucifer had sidestepped and flew right behind me before pushing me forward to face the giant, beautiful, and oh so angry, Owl of Craftsmanship.

"Why have you awakened me at this hour Lucifer? Surely you realize that I am a nocturnal creature, *Boy*." The voice of the owl was strong and firm, but it held the tone of peace and justice. Now that he's awoken, I took notice of his face, and where his pupils should have been, were nothing but glowing white light that seemed to give off a mystical mist.

"Boy? Really Rústicar, you're only a millennia older than myself. Barely I might add." Lucifer cackled and pointed my way. *"Anyways, as was agreed, HE is escaping and my forces are barely back to what they were all those years ago."* Lucy informed, his voice wavering. That was a shock, the mighty lord of hell himself, seemed to be stricken with fear at whatever this new threat was. The great owl reached past both of us with his large talons, big enough to stab through a horse long ways.

"Oh, where are those spectacles?" He murmured, before finally locating them. He adjusted the large eyewear on his face and took a long gander at me. **"You're telling me that this boy is the one I prophesied so long ago?"** Rústicar asked with dread. **"He can't be more than a century old..."** he paused before reeling back and squawking at me. **"WHAT IS THIS!? YOU DARE BRING A DEMON HERE!? IN MY PRESENCE!?"** Extending his wings, and neck at me in an aggressive fashion, I stood ready to withstand whatever he threw at me. Being as ancient as he is, there was nothing that I would be able to do to stop such an attack, other than face it head on.

Lucifer and Katrina stood off to the side watching for what would happen, their warriors holding weapons out, to keep me from running. Rústicar was still flaring his wings in a threatening manner screeching at me. A mighty flap of his wings caused hurricane force winds to whip around us, chains whipping and thrashing the walls, making it hard to stand my ground without slightly shifting my weight or ducking.

Well come on you damn bird, it's now or never if I hope to get answers. Rústīcar gave off a final squawk before charging me with talons bared. If this is how I die, then so be it.

Closing my eyes, I waited for the pain that I knew was inevitable, yet... it never came. I heard heaving right in front of me, his breath hot against my face. Opening my eyes, I saw glowing chains anchoring his neck to keep him from coming any closer. Orange and blue light merged as symbols emerged all around the room, glowing with ancient power. The chains strapped to Rústīcar glowed a deep orange before pulling him back to his spot in the nest. He was a strong being, but the power he had and knew he was able to use was... muffled. Rústīcar eyed me angrily, trying to force his way back to me but the chains held firm and strong. Within seconds, he was back in his spot... imprisoned.

From behind me, there was a low clapping.

"Well done Janix, you've held your ground, though I must say that I wasn't expecting such a dramatic performance from Rústīcar." Lucifer said from behind me before going on, *"As you can see, he is imprisoned and the collar around his neck inhibits his true powers."*

"And if it wasn't for these damn chains, I would tear you limb from limb, *Janix.*" Rústīcar screeched. **"Now, why did you bring a demon to me,** *Devil.*"

"Janix, show him." Lucifer said.

With a raised eyebrow, I extended my black and white wings, exposing my mixed blood. Rústīcar once again screeched at me. He realized what I was and still didn't like it.

"So it's worse than I had feared then..." Rústīcar stated, to which I just frowned and asked.

"Worse than you feared?"

Rústīcar and Lucifer shared a look while Katrina stood to the side whispering orders to her subordinates who scurried off with haste .

"*Janix, have you an idea where you are?*" Lucifer asked. With a shake of my head, he continued.

"I sent my son to meet you, I informed Dehaas that it would be in all of our best interests to have you sent to this forest. I needed you to be here for the sake of this existence." Lucifer began cryptically. "There are things in this world that you couldn't fathom… even with your century of life."

Frowning, "What do you mean?"

"*Janix… it's time for you to learn about what's going on down in hell, and it's time that you understand your true place in Fathers plan. Having to fight Michael will feel like child's play compared to who is stirring. It is time reveal your true purpose in this world… Why you're still alive! Why Father brought you back… It's time for you to embrace your true destiny.*"

CHAPTER 6

True Evil Revealed

The secondary location, a contingency plan set in place should things go awry for either of us and we needed to find each other. This is the location I must get to. Then the other lords and I will be able conduct planning for a response to our next course of action. But first, I have to endure whatever it is that Lucifer, Katrina, and this humongous Owl have to tell me. Though, I am intrigued, for Lucifer himself is afraid, and Katrina has said very little since he showed up and took the lead... until now...

"Janix, you are in the forest of Īzenük, an ancient forest almost as old as the garden of Eden itself. Not only that, but it's also home to the hidden gates of hell." Katrina stated.

"But why and how did you get here?" After we escaped, neither Ailani or I were able to track Katrina down. It was as if she was never even on this earth.

Sighing, "I was a spy working against the Angelic army long before you ever showed up. Working with Andreas and Dehaas as their personal informant. Then with the information, they would sabotage what they could without getting caught, any defectors who wanted to leave but didn't want to fight, they sent here; to my forest." She explained, "After you and my sister escaped, I had to disappear, which is when I met this merchant, warlock and she demon. I believe their names were... Smee and Albright. Anyways, I got directions to a location with very little inhabitants and they pointed me this way." This all made a little sense now, but that still left the question; how is she the queen, as that's all that crown could mean?

"And the crown?"

"You could say that I… may have made a deal with a devil." She stated blushing and casting her eyes downward. Lucifer sent me a wink when she finished making me shudder. Dear lord… Oh dear lord, of all the beings…

"THE Devil, my dear. Although there are other creatures who go by the description and claim the title, I am in fact the one and only Devil. For I'm the only one who thought to question my father's choices, and for it he punished me in doing so." Lucifer cut in smugly.

"So… you made a deal with Lucy here and, what? You became queen?" I asked still slightly confused.

"Great Nox help me!" Rústīcar griped, bringing a wing to his face, as if face palming and letting out a huff in anguish.

"The boy doesn't even understand a demonic deal? Lucifer! Does he know anything of what is to come? More importantly, is he even trained for what is to come!?" Rústīcar asked. The Lord of Sin, riddled me with his sheepish expression to the cryptic question at hand.

"Not at all Rústīcar."

"And what of the priestess? I believe you called her Alberta?" Rústīcar asked, while trying to think about the next plan for whatever it is I'm suppose to be ready for.

"Taken by Arkain and Dehaas." Lucifer replied. *"Ailani is pregnant with a mortals child, as such, it had to be taken care of."* Lucy explained to Rústīcar. *"Everything should be taken care of within… the next, maybe three hours."*

"Very well, if that is the case then I suppose its time for us to introduce this ones trai…"

"Wait a minute!" I exclaimed. "Take care of the kid??? What do you mean!?"

"Although her powers lay dormant, she cannot utilize them to their maximum potential until the child, which drains her of strength, mana and mental fortitude, is removed." Rústīcar explained.

"I've been keeping an eye; through other eyes on the happenings of the world... As well as being brought up to speed by Lucifer and Katrina."

"Y'all make it sound like you're going to get rid of the child all together?!" I questioned.

"That is essentially the idea, yes." Katrina jumped in. Looking at her, "You can't be serious? Surely you're not on board with killing your own nephew or niece?" I couldn't believe what I was hearing, this is a life, not something to be snuffed out; like that of a candles flame.

"You think I like the idea of having to kill my sister's child!? This pains me more than I would like to admit. But if we wish to save the world from being razed, then yes, I will sacrifice the child if it brings about the means to save the lives of the earth.

"NO! THERE HAS TO BE ANO..."

"*THAT'S ENOUGH, JANIX!*" Lucifer exclaimed, the lights in the room dimming again, shadows closing around us until it was only us two together. Lucifer snapped his fingers and red chains fastened themselves to my arms and legs. A collar that glowed orange wrapped around my neck like that of Rústīcar's. I tried to fight it, pulling with all my strength but... I was unable to use any of my supernatural power, I was weak, I was vulnerable, I was mortal.

"You think that beating Michael was your greatest challenge, BOY!" Lucifer seethed before materializing out of the shadows in front of me. "Keep in mind, though Michael was the better warrior, and I may not be back to my full power after the last battle when IT almost killed me, I am far stronger than my dear BROTHER!" Lucifer ranted before back handing me across the face. It was like I was hit by the force of ten hurricanes before he snapped his fingers again making the chains pull me down into a kneeling position.

"You think you can face this next challenge with the sentiment of a pathetic mortal?" The surrounding shadows morphed around his head until dissipating at the Hellfire crown now sitting upon his morphing skull. His flesh disintegrating, which allowed long horns to grow from his temples. His eyes sunk into his now fleshless skull, leaving hollow unending blackness in their place. A wicked smile of sharpening teeth replaced his calm and collected appearance. His suit burned into a tunic formed by the tormented souls of the damned.

"Then, you may as well surrender your life here and now!" An obsidian black sword rose out of the shadows in front of myself.

Manipulating the shadows to allow shapes and figures to appear, a scene cast before me. We were now in a large expanse of burning vegetation, destroyed buildings littered the area. Around us were creatures torn limb from limb, strewn all around the land scape. Before me, was the burning corpses of villagers. Véchenti forest, was no more.

"For what you face, will use that against you, then manipulate you into oblivion." Grabbing my head, and making me look forward, past the expanse, my eyes widened as dread began to take over. Fear and dread began to fill me as I once again tried to struggle against the bonds that held me. There was a large shadow, as tall as a mountain and held enough malice to fill one. It's steps were soundless, however, I knew that was only because of the shadows. In one quick thought, I knew that if I was really in the presence of this beast, then I would die. I watched as the hulking blob of grey stepped over us.

Then as quickly as it came, the darkness began to evaporate until we were back in Rústícar's room.

"What just happened Janix, may have only been an illusion, but what you just witnessed, is a very real future that may come to pass... He is returning to the mortal world, and with him... DEATH! As

weak as you are now, you'd stand no chance to defeat such an ancient evil." Lucifer explained.

"Then why even show me? Why even bring me here if there is no hope?" I asked, my voice wavering.

Lucifer snapped his fingers allowing the chains and collar to dissipate. I was breathing heavily, the shock of such an evil being, the likes of which I'd never seen before, setting in.

"Because you have us, you have allies, and you have Ailani to help you." Katrina stated with a light smile, trying to offer me some comfort. Completely contrast to how I was received when getting here. Lucifer continued, "*This will be the fight to end all fights, the survivors will never be the same, the dead will be too numerous to count. But there is a prophecy, one that states you and a priestess will lead us all, into salvation.*" I understood what they were telling me. Once again, I was a pawn to the Lords twisted game of life... death, and chess. But there was still one nagging question that I refused to leave unanswered...

"What... What was that horrid monster?" I asked, finally calming my nerves. I didn't understand! I wasn't even in the real things presence, but it was enough to leave me stricken with fear! Lucifer nodded to the grim look I had, recognizing that I now understood how bad this next fight would be.

"**He is known by many names, and just as many titles. But there are three that stand out amongst the rest.**" Rústīcar answered, "**Tiléqan; The harbinger of death... Victēncy; The creator of chaos... Anubisety; The ender of worlds... But the most famous of names... Cûrburõs... The Final Trinity.**"

CHAPTER 7

Saving a Child

"Cûrburõs," I whispered the name, it's weight heavy on my tongue. The magnitude of this threat is something greater than I once thought it was, something which will require much more than an alliance of supernatural powers. This will be even greater than the Reckoning war. I understand why we need Ailani to be at her full strength, still… I didn't like the idea of the sacrificing an innocent child for the sake of our survival… That goes against everything we fought for… not to mention, Ailani would never forgive me, that is assuming that she didn't kill everyone involved in the death of her child. However, this also gave me an idea, it will still be painful for Ailani who potentially will never see her child again. But they are angels… right?

"Lucifer, Rústícar, what if… what if instead of killing the unborn child, the angels age it?" This got a look of interest from both of them and even Katrina looked up, interested in such an idea.

"For the sake of the mission, we need Ailani to be in her prime, in order for her to realize her true powers… the child must go!" I said through grit teeth. "But did y'all ever think about how it would affect her mentally?" I asked, pointing to my own head to emphasis the point.

"*She'll get over it, why waste the time.*" A nonchalant Lucifer replied. I lost him, and Katrina simply offered me a slight smile at my efforts, but then she also turned away. My face fell slightly,

I was about to retort once again until Rústīcar held up a large wing.

"Come now Lucifer, surely even you're interested in such an outlandish idea? I must say, if he were anyone else, then they would just sulk and be depressed about what they could not change. Letting the child die without even trying to push any real idea of saving it."

"I won't disagree with you, Rústīcar, but still, that'll take more energy than necessary. Why not kill the child and be done with it?" Lucifer answered with a bored expression. Rústīcar burst out laughing, it was a deep methodic laugh, one that seemed to resonate around the room before he calmed down.

"You and I both know that Andreas and Dehaas have the ability to do it safely and quickly, yes it will take some extra divine energy, but, let's hear out what the boy has to say." Rústīcar said wiggling his owlish eyebrows.

"I agree with Rústīcar," Katrina chimed in. "As Ailani's blood sister, I can understand the emotional pain that she will be in, Lucifer... love, can't we just hear out what Janix is trying to get at?" She looked to the Lord of Hell with pleading eyes. I couldn't help but snicker at Lucy's look of defeat. Until he finally sighed and waved his hand for me to continue. Who knew that Katrina would have such an affect on the Lord of Hell? I'll need to speak with her later though.

"Go on boy, you have all of our attention now. Finish what you're getting at." With an owlish eyebrow raised he waited, glowing white, electric blue and crimson red eyes burning a hole into my soul. He was allowing me this one chance to save Ailani's child, I couldn't waste it.

"In the times of old, the lord's son, his mother was a virgin right? Well, why not just... speed the aging process up a little faster. Age the child to be born say... tomorrow," listening intently, Rústīcar seemed to be going into deeper thought. "then take it somewhere safe. Ailani will hate the idea, but its a better outcome than… the latter." I stated to the trio who appeared to all be in a heated mental debate with themselves. So I decided to give them more incentive to save the child.

"I will not allow her child to be murdered, not without having the chance to experience its first breath of life. To experience the world for all its beauty."

"Why are you so persistent for one child… One of which isn't even yours?" Katrina asked breaking the silence.

"My child or not, I will be its guardian if need be. I swear it! I also swear, that if y'all murder this innocent life, then I will do everything in my power to make sure you fade out of existence! Even if it kills me." I finished strong and full of passion. This was the truth, if they wouldn't listen to reason with the idea of me taking the child under my wing, then Cûrburõs or no Cûrburõs I will threaten war… this planet be damned. My threat hung in the air, the room was suddenly tense and silent. It was clear that they had never been threatened by a mortal like me before.

The silence in the room was intense, if a drop of water were to fall and splatter on the floor, I have no doubt that it would have been heard. All three of them seemed to be deep in thought; until, Rústĩcar's eyes began glowing brighter to the point of getting blinding. He raised his massive beaked head to the ceiling, remained like this for a few moments, before looking back at me. In his dialect, he began slow chanting in the language of the old owl. It was a language ancient and full of power, the walls illuminated blue again, but… red and green characters appeared this time. The collar, unlike the first time when he attempted to attack me, didn't glow this time. Snapping his head towards me, the light dimmed and until a red mist slowly fell from his great beak.

"Understand that we have heard your pleas boy," Rústĩcar said breaking me out of stupor. The mist landing at the base of his talons and spreading along the ground. **"Understand that**

I have heard your reasoning, leave us now. We have much to discuss." He said waving me off with a massive wing.

"Janix, I do believe that there is a certain Lord waiting for you outside." Katrina called after me. Nodding my head with hope and a little confusion, I backed off. At this point, all I could do was wait for the decision, one that would decide if I am once again, forced to choose between a certain group for the sake of the world.

As the large doors closed behind me, I was suddenly attacked by a huge fluff of fur and a slobbery tongue. Laughing, I tried to push the over sized puppy hellhound, I knew as Steefas, off of me.

"Ok, Ok! My friend. You're going to suffocate me in licks and wolf hugs."

"Master, when you never made it back to the location, we all assumed the worst. We've sent scouts everywhere looking for you and Ailani..." He paused as if realizing now that she wasn't with me. "Master?" He asked getting off of me.

"She's with the Angels... Steefas, how are you here and do you know where we are?" I asked. I still wasn't entirely sure myself, as all I was given was a name.

"Īzenük forest. I was just a pup at the time, but it's an Ancient forest created before the garden of Eden, Hiding place for the gates of hell, and ancient battle field to which so many lost their lives so long ago. Andreas flew into our chambers, which is also where I left the other lords, he informed us of a plight that is rising, and that a surprise awaited me." Well, I guess I'm not that surprised that Steefas would know about this place... or that Andreas was willing to throw me a bone... fuck, my head is going to be throbbing before the end of this day.

"By the smell of the place, I'd wager that Katrina and Lucifer have been mates for a while now." I nodded thinking on other things until something stood out.

"Wait! Don't tell me you can smell... Damn it Steefas! We seriously need to teach you about things that shouldn't be said over things that should." Steefas simply gave me a wolfish grin as I palmed my face in annoyance.

"Anyways, we have a big problem, things are not going to be as simple as we once thought and we need to end these skirmishes with the angels immediately." With a raised eyebrow, Steefas waited for me to continue.

"The world is in danger, more than enslavement, this time, it appears that we could be looking at world wide annihilation…"

"Soooo, dramatic master!" Steefas replied laughing. "Though in my years of life, I can acknowledge the other beings who reside in the world. Beings such as the shapeshifters of old, to the Lycans who are a newer breed." I nodded, accepting what he was getting at, however he still didn't grasp what I was saying.

"We've also fought against most creatures in-order to survive while Michael was coming into power. Not to include fighting Michael himself." Steefas stated, still looking at me. His goodnatured smile and mirth left when he saw my ashen face.

"This is something worse… isn't it?" Steefas asked, ears falling flush against his wolfish head.

"You could say tha…" I began but was interrupted by a loud bang as the door was pulled open by Katrina.

In the center of the room, wrapped in white linen with golden trimming, was a sleeping Ailani. She appeared to be at peace, though… the stress was plainly obvious and painted all over her face. Bags were under her eyes as she was appeared to be exhausted. Not only this, but it appeared that she was no longer pregnant. Her round belly now flush against her physically fit body again. This only meant one thing, which; filled my face with sadness, dread and anger. Thoughts that we had been too late filled my mind… That is, until another angel landed lightly, it was a veiled woman, holding a living and breathing child in her arms, Ailani's new daughter had been born. The new life had been saved.

CHAPTER 8

Janix, Guardian of a newborn

"Janix!" Andreas called, nodding to Steefas who trailed behind me. "you owe all of us a hardy night of drinks, it's been over two thousand years since we've had to use divine magic such as this for a second time within two years just to ensure the child survived his birth." Andreas walked over to me clasping my forearm with his and pulling me into a brotherly hug, I was taken aback by this until he leaned into my ear.

"There is much that we must talk about, if the girl is to live and prosper, you must train her, then leave her. Find me tonight." He whispered cryptically into my ear before pulling back. I nodded in understanding before focusing on a groaning Ailani. Steefas walked up to her before giving her a sniff. At his nod that she was ok he and I looked to the Angel who was holding the baby.

'Is that the child?' Steefas telepathically asked.

"Janix!" Boomed the voice of Rústīcar, "You claimed that you would become the Childs protector, and you shall." With a talion he lightly touched the forehead of the baby. "From this day forth, you are her guardian. May she live and prosper under your tutelage. Also, tomorrow you will train under new teachers, tomorrow you and Lord Steefas will obtain the knowledge needed to assist you in the battles to come." Rústīcar nodded to Katrina who picked up her still groaning sister and gave me a nod before leaving. "In three days' time, she will begin training her powers to make them stronger than they were in the battle with Michael." Rústīcar finished before rotating his head behind him so he didn't have to look at us anymore.

Lucifer waited for Katrina to leave with Ailani before addressing the she-angel and walking over to me.

"Alright Janix, remember, this is your responsibility now." He said gesturing to the child, Steefas stood behind me listening intently. He would want an explanation to what had transpired this day. "Everyday Dehaas, Andreas or I will come and age the girl." You are responsible for teaching her how to live, how to fight, and how to survive."

"How old will she be when y'all finally stop?"

"Approximately... ten, maybe twelve depending on how comprehensive she is." Lucifer stated before whispering to the angel.

Taking off her vail, my hand instinctively shot for my machete which was still nowhere be found. I recognized this woman, she was no angel...

"This, is Roving Angel Bella, you should remember her, she was originally one of my top Knights of Hell before meeting you." I did remember, during the **Reckoning**, we had met briefly and she even almost killed me once.

"Trust me Lucifer, we are well acquainted." I said with narrowed eyes before eyeing her clothing. It was then that I noticed her curved and poisoned blades she always had on her waist.

"Still got those evil things?" I asked, earning a grin from Bella.

"Are you still sour about that duel?" She asked with a raised eyebrow.

"Not the duel itself," I said softly, she was a skilled fighter, one whose skills are worthy of praise. "However, I still have the scars you gave me. The cuts which would have done me in, had Lucas not known a cure for your poison." I replied slightly bitter, as I tentatively chest where the long scar began. This earned a possessive growl from Steefas. I thought back to the time Ailani commented about my scarred chest, and having so many wounds.

"Well if it's any consolation, I'm glad I didn't kill you." She whispered, slyly batting her eyes flirtatiously at me, I shivered slightly as I thought about what she was implicating, she really is one of Lucifers followers.

"Yeah well, so am I Bella." I replied.

"She will also be watching over the child with you." I blanched at that statement.

"You can't be serious? You want her helping me with... does the child have a name?" I asked, realizing that we've been calling it 'the child' this whole time.

"Call it what you wish, it matters not to me." Lucifer replied, "Now! I have to continue fortifying my kingdom known as Hell." Extending his black wings, he took off through a portal in the ceiling before leaving me to our devises.

"So the child has no name then? Nor does it have any parentage to speak of right now." Stated a vary curious Steefas. Looking at her sleeping in Bella's arms, I couldn't help but smile. It really was cruel, having to take the child from its mother and not be raised properly... A cruel fate indeed. Sighing, I looked at the child.

"May I?" I asked holding out my arms, to which Bella gently gave me the girl.

I've never had a problem with children, nor have I ever had a problem with babies, however, I've never had the pleasure of being around one long enough to hold one in my arms. That's the price of being the best at what I did, to include being the final surviving agent of the Lord.

"Hey there little one," I whispered, smiling, Ailani's little girl, "I have no doubt that you'll grow up to be as beautiful as your mother one day." I said thinking back to when Alex first asked for my permission to marry Ailani. I was so happy when he did, I knew she would be out of harm's way. So of course I said yes... though, it still stung when I sat in the back, drinking a flask of whiskey. Yearning for something that was never meant to be, I congratulated the two and left the wedding, making the excuse that Steefas and I had business to take care of. Grabbing a bottle of whiskey, Steefas readily agreed, not liking the amount of sadness rolling off me like a river. The rest of the night was a blur, one that I barely remember, other then waking up with two bottles of liquor at my feet and a sleeping Steefas keeping me locked with in my own house.

"What are we going to call you young one." I asked aloud as I let Steefas sniff her.

"She will be a strong woman, one that will no doubt be the Alpha female to the family she starts." Laughing lightly, I knew that it was way too early to be thinking like that. But it was still nice to hear.

"No doubt about that man." I thought too, when Alex announced that he and Ailani were expecting, it was an amazing day. I treated them to some of the best food one could get, cooked by a couple of Gin who amusingly enough, had one hell of a skill for cooking. They talked about names and what they would call it, should the child be either boy or girl. Then as one, we all seemed to agree with Dänai—meaning beautiful one— or Jeylac— meaning strength of Gods.

"Welcome to the world, little Dänai." I said, earning a little coo from baby Nae.

"So Nix, what's our plan now?" Bella asked who now put her hands behind her head, now that her wings were retracted.

"Don't call me Nix, and there is no our. You're just here to help watch over Nae."

"Oh don't be like that Nix, with our history, think of what we can accomplish." She said giggling like a little school girl, until a deep growl was heard behind her.

"Master said not to call him Nix, KNIGHT!" Steefas gutturally growled.

"Easy Steefas, despite her docile look, she would still be more than a handful for you, not to mention we still need a baby sitter whenever I'm doing whatever it is Rústī-car has in mind." Steefas quit growling but kept his hackles raised.

"Down fitto." Bella cackled before following me and the child. Steefas took the rear, mentally grumbling about cocky Knights of Hell. These next few months would be rough ones, especially with Bella working with me now... Katrina came back letting us know that they had two other rooms waiting to be occupied. This would have been good news, however, Bella just had to make it complicated. Stated that she wouldn't go anywhere without the child and I wasn't about to trust Nae being out of my sight, at least not tonight. So when Bella insisted on staying in the same room, I finally conceded, asking for extra cushions and making a bed on the floor. Steefas curled around me, providing warmth. The room having been modified for his extra horse size, allowed all of us comfort as little Nae slept in a crib. Silent and happy, one thought couldn't leave my mind though... Bella, the former Knight of Hell will be the death of me.

CHAPTER 9

Surviving knight

June 20th, 2022
In Hell before Ailani was taken

Beneath the seven gateways of hell, protected by the gatekeeper Sérran, were legions upon legions of demons who armed themselves for survival. Not only did the Hell-spawn arm themselves, but weapons were also offered to the eternally damned, fighting in exchange for freedom. This is what the tortured souls were offered, should they assist in the fight... and survive the war.

All of Hell was preparing for war, though... not for a war with the angels, nor was it for a war with another army... No! Hell itself was full of desolate plains which consisted of black, jagged, burning and sharp bedrock. Mineral that would cut anyone to bits and leave them shredded. Even the thickest of leather garments wouldn't stop the stone from cutting skin. Rivers of magma flowing into a lake of molten fire, constantly shifting and swirling beneath the known world. Waves of magma crashed on the bedrock, melting it and adding to the sea beneath the earth's crust, melting and solidifying the banks of the stone cove. But around a crevice that extended deeper into the uncharted places of Hell, were the walls of Lucifer's fortress. Constructed of volcanic rock, towers stood tall, overlooking each of its walls. They were thick and strong with the bodies of innocents, used as cementing blocks to hold them together. It is a mighty fortress, one built with the intention of withstanding any threat that the world could throw at it. Be that threat physical or spiritual, this fortress was the only thing keeping something more ancient than the angels themselves, at bay...

However, it was never going to be enough... the veteran demons know, those who survived the first battle anyway. They understand the weight that even hell spawn must carry, the severity of the beast they prepare to face. The virtuous know of what it is, to work side by side, with all the other beings in the world, and still have little to no chance at winning in the battles to come. They also know... that they stand no chance against an evil such as this. Nor will the fortress withstand such a threat.

Even now, there are Knights of Hell who descended into the desolate pit. Knights who are fighting for their lives by Lucifer's order. It was a routine mission to ensure that the collars are securely strapped to *its* three necks. However... the mission in which they were sent for did not go well. Wielding enhanced weaponry, from angelically blessed swords and arrows which were originally owned by former Angels, to cursed blades bathed in the blood of young innocents, they had descended into the pit. They had black chest pieces made of solid steel, taken from the bodies of those in the above world. On their arms and legs were gauntlets and shinguards made of mammoth bone. The helms, adorned with furs around the skulls of goat heads, making them appear to not be of human origin. Of the one thousand; hardened, tormented, demonically blessed and trained **Knights of Hell** who were sent into the pit, roughly four hundred remained. Battered and maimed, the remaining knights rode for their lives. All of them on steeds of Hell fire, attempted to return to Lucifer before something inevitable happened. If not for the current leader of the Knights, RÿJunìc, who ordered them to pull out of the pit, none of them would have survived.

In Hell after Ailani is taken

The Hell-spawn who manned the towers, blew their horns alerting all of Hell to the returning Knights. Riding into Lucifer's fortress of towers, RÿJunìc stopped in front of the steps to the main entrance and dismounted his steed Klivoer. He ran into the tower as an echoing sound of chains snapping shook all of hell, causing the upper world's forest to shake. Anti-mater leaked into the atmosphere. This phenomenon causing lightning storms and hellish weather to take place in the forest of Īzenük, and a loud roar sounded as the creature trapped below, bellowed in rage. Six glowing eyes leered through the darkness as a single Knight who remained behind brandished a flaming sword in defiance, yelling as he met his final fate; consumed by the jaws of the three headed hound. Tearing him into three pieces, the one head which was now free from the chains that bound it, laughed in evil mirth. Bones of the knight crunched as the hound's rows of teeth rotated, grinding together until nothing was left.

Lucifer peered out of his tower window, observing the event that took place, when he sensed someone enter his chambers. "What news do you bring me from the pit, RÿJunìc?" He asked turning to the knight as RÿJunìc kneeled at Lucifers feet. His shredded armor strained against his muscles, blood dripping from his wounded head as the straps threatened to fall off.

With a deep and strained voice, RÿJunìc replied. "My lord, our forces were decimated, the chains grow weak, and the collars are failing. My lord, I'm sorry." With his head hung low, locks of long brunette hair fell in front of his tanned face. He awaited Lucifers judgement. If a Knight of Hell were to fail his mission, it was a punishment worst than death; to be put back on the lines of torment and then branded a failure. Every night, the Knight would then be sodomized with cacti and finally blood eagled in front of the entire legion.

47

Lucifer sighed, "Rise warrior, it is no surprise that you failed, as I did not anticipate you succeeding if any-thing was amiss. Prepare the rest of the Knights, I must go and let the great owl know of what is to come. Also, it is time for Janix to understand what is to happen now." Extending his black wings, Lucifer called upon some of his followers from the times of old, before opening a portal which would create a crevice in the throne room of Katrina.

After Lucifer left, RÿJunìc stood shaking his head. His master was kind to not issue out a punishment for him, he thought, ripping the already mangled armor off. This exposed his large and toned chest as he walked through the tower to his section where the Knights resided. However, in that conversation, RÿJunìc learned two things... One, Lord Lucifer knew it was a suicide mission that cost him hundreds of good unholy warriors... and two, they had no chance of standing up to this being, if the way he spoke was anything to go by.

Upon arriving at the Knights Barracks, he called for Casdriant. A small and sickly looking demon with a caved in head and jagged teeth sauntered up to him with a stone tablet in hand. "Get me a status report on the wounded, how many do we have left, and what gear must be replaced. Get me this information within the next two hours, I'm going to bathe, anyone able is allowed to do the same."

"Yes, my lord!" Casdriant replied extending his right arm in salute before leaving to check on the other warriors. He took account of lost warriors, lost gear, and what they would have to do in-order to ensure that they even stood a chance at surviving the next battle.

RÿJunìc stripped off his clothing, dropping each article in a line as he walked into the boiling water that was provided, remembering the mission... It wasn't just some battle that took place... It was a massacre... one that had been costly, and now all he, and the rest of hell could do was hope... hope that the remaining chains which bound Cûrburõs withstood the trials of time until a better solution was found. The next few hours that they would gain to rest was sure to be some of the last that he and the other knights would be allowed for a long while.

And so... in the pits of Hell itself, Hope was abandoned...

CHAPTER 10

Headaches of a Devil

Lucifer after leaving Rústīcar' prison

Screams, cries, begging, pleading for mercy! These are the sounds that plagued the mind of Lucifer, visions of torture, dismemberment, and eternal suffering for the men and women who've been condemned. The mind of Satan, Lord of Hell, Lord of Sin itself, the epitome of Evil, Lucifer; the Fallen Angel, who always dressed in such classy attire and relished in the misery of others, was in a jam. As even Lucifer wasn't prideful enough to think he'd come out of these final years on earth, as everyone knows it, unscathed.

After the meeting in Rústīcar' chambers had concluded, Lucifer flew into the portal, knowing that once he exited on the other side of the mountains, he'd probably have to fix a number of problems in the forest of Véchenti. However; this was not the case, upon exiting the portal, he was greeted by a procession of hell hounds 'Steefas' children' who were patrolling the battle worn streets. Aside from the dead warriors struck down with angelic weapons protruding from limbs, skulls and chests, as well as the dead contingent of Angels, all seemed to be under control. The hell hounds assisted with gathering the dead, or comforting children with no family left in the embraces of their soft fur.

At his own feet was a dead child, its head caved in from what looks like a long rod. Most likely an angelic javelin was the culprit, an eye was popped out of its sunken socket as bits of skull lay strewn about the land at his feet, brain matter trickled out of its ears. All in all, the remains of the child looked nothing more than that of ground beef. The civilians and warriors that had fallen didn't look any better... though, even with all the gore around him, Lucifer felt... nothing. To Lucifer, it was just another example of why humanity wasn't worth keeping around... even if he had a select few that he favored—you know, Katrina and Janix— he felt no anger, no pity. The lord of hell was hollow to these emotions, at least... he was, that is until he felt this overpowering urge to look away overtook him. The scene before him, it was too much... even for the Lord of Hell, he didn't like the look... it, was a foreign feeling but it was there nonetheless.

"That Katrina is going to ruin me..." he stated to no one in particular as he did his best to brush off the odd sensation of disgust. Observing everything happening from his position, it wasn't but a few moments before he was noticed by Egnachi, Steefas' wiener dog offspring who broke him from his thoughts.

"My lord!" Egnachi exclaimed trotting up, it was quite the amusing sight. "Why would you come to this for-saken forest?"

"Forsaken you say?" Lucifer asked in confusion, from what he understood, and what his spies had relayed back to him, things were bad but not that bad. The attack which took place was quickly expunged by the Hellhound Lord's children. The other lords; such as the Lycan king, village Elder and other commanders were taken to a forti-fied location under the city. So what could possibly make them say something so rash?

"Yes Lord Lucifer, as you can see." The Wiener dog turned away from him, pointing to one of the homes that a hell hound entered with the consent of the villagers as they stayed outside with their children.

"It looks as if you're searching for something?" This made Egnachi grimace.

"The battle was a ferocious one. It seemed as if the Angelic faction was almost desperate to die, they refused to yield... anyways, when we showed up, Dehaas and Andreas were up to their necks in the factions attacking unit and there were already a number of dead angels, gin and other creatures at their feet." Egnachi sighed, "This is when we joined the fight. We lost so many of my brothers and sisters," Egnachi stated solemnly "all who have returned to the shadows now, not to mention how many villagers lost their lives... we are now assisting in the search of the dead... like that girl by your feet."

"Yes... I did notice that the death toll appeared to be quite high, before now, the remaining factions who re-fused to acknowledge Dehaas as the Lord over the silver city never assaulted towns." Lucifer stated before making himself look upon the gore once again. "Who was she?"

"I believe uncle Nix called her... *Amelia*, the sister survived and is somewhere in the masses" Lucifer blanched at that. Amelia? That Amelia, Lucifer was in total shock, for there was only one Amelia in this village. This was her, this was the girl that Janix was personally training, turning into a warrior and his potential replacement as a general for the future... Damn...

"My Lord? Are you feeling alright?" Asked a very concerned Egnachi. Seeing that everything seemed to be handled though, I opened a portal before addressing Egnachi one last time.

"You're saying this child is the girl Janix *was* training... if that's the case, then my father helped those involved," Lucifer knew exactly how Janix was with his friends. He will appear calm, but in the end... Janix was nothing more than a ticking bomb whose fuse just needed to be cut at the right time and then... well... **even y'all reading this story know how that will end.** "Let the lords know that he and Ailani are well, and under the protection of primordial beings, as well as your father who is with Janix now." With that, he extended his wings and flew through the portal, disappearing once again into the night sky.

On the other side of the portal, Lucifer's mind was so full of turmoil and catastrophe as well as visions of future suffering. So deep in thought that he didn't realize that he was back in the chambers of Katrina Spirit. Yet, he was right to be in such a distracted state of mind, as the events playing out right now were all indicators of higher forces at work, and for all of his malicious manipulations of humanity, begrudgingly, even Lucifer had to admit that there is nothing he'd be able to do if the greater evil was unleashed upon the world. So knowing that he left Janix and the girl's newborn child in the care of his second most trusted Knight, Bella, put even his sinful mind at ease. Especially knowing the toll that Amelia's death was about to take on Janix.

CLAP!!!

Lucifer was brought out of his thoughts as Katrina clapped right in front of his face, "Lucy... are you alright? You were out of it for a few minutes." Lucifer nodded his head, grinning at the nickname she gave him before looking at the bed and seeing the sleeping form of Ailani Spirit... the girl he'd love nothing more than to have her memories wiped again and her child killed.

"So much has changed, in the millennium I've lived Katrina..." Lucifer stated while looking back at his lover. "That's what happens when time passes and you try to avoid the affections of us *mortals*." She drawled sarcastically, a sly smirk gracing her lips. Scoffing, Lucifer snapped his fingers allowing his garments too morph into that of his dress suit.

"I used to be the most vile creation the world has ever known," Lucifer stated, his eyes turning a solid shade of crimson. His voice deepened, taking on the ancient power that he chose to keep dormant. "The kind of creature that you sacrifice your children to, the kind you PRAY... never sets it gaze on you."

Two Long horns grew out of his temples and a long lengthy tail slowly slithered from the hid-den hole in his nice dress trousers.

Katrina rolled her eyes before chuckling, "Well aren't we moody today." Moving away from the bed, Katrina sighed before looking to her fallen Angel of a boyfriend. "Let us occupy the other chambers, allow her some peace before the rest of the world falls on her... again."

Nodding, Lucifer followed her lead, steam began to come off his body, the leathery skin that he took on while going into his king of hell appearance morphed back to that of a tall muscular man with black angel wings. Then, even his wings returned into his back, hiding themselves, before his horns finally receded into his temples.

"I always forget that you have more than one room for *your* clothing." Lucifer stated as Katrina walked up to a mannequin, stripping herself of the armor and placing it on the respective ligament of the mannequin's body.

Lucifer recalled the agonizing process of all the scheming with his father—*Yes, you heard right, scheming, Lucifer's dramatic efforts of the Reckoning war in which he waged was not his own decision, but a request from his father*— who was the one to set these events in motion. That is, until the Lord himself chose to leave the known world, disappearing until even the Angels couldn't find him... yet Janix... this *MORTAL!* He was the one who spoke to Satan's father before vanishing off the face of the earth, only to show himself to Andreas—**Lucifer's own son** — and Dehaas.

"What's the point in being queen if I can't take advantage of... certain privileges it affords me." She smiled as she finished taking off the armor and untying the binds that held her leather garments up. She released the binding, allowing them to fall to the ground soundless as she turned to look at him, hands on her hips and standing in her unclothed glory.

Lucifer laughed, "Privileges indeed. Now, there is a number things that have happened?" Walking towards him, she drew her diamond sword from its sheath on the mannequin.

"Very well, but first," she threw her sword like a spear at him which Lucifer caught at the hilt with ease and only a slight tilt of his head. "Put that away behind you please?" She said before turning around and sifting through a drawer for something.

"Now what would you have done if I hadn't caught the blade, or it impaled me?" Lucifer asked before sliding it into the spared sheath which hung on a wall.

"I'd be pissed at you for dropping my blade and have to ask Janix to kick your ass," she said, surprising him with a tender embrace. "you understand that... though you may have caught him off guard tonight, he does possess enough strength to kill even you right?" She replied quietly, almost with a hint of worry before leaning her head on his back, Lucifer sat in silence, thinking.

"I know Katrina... hell, if it weren't for those chains and the collar, then I surely, wouldn't have stood a chance against him... but we'll see how he takes the news about the death of one of his apprentices." he stated before grabbing Katrina's robe from next to the sword. Turning around in her arms, he leaned his forehead against hers, draping it around her.

Katrina gave him a quizzical look to which he explained all that he witnessed and was informed of. However, nothing would prepare them for the years ahead, the last two years that will only get harder every day they thrive. Everything, is about to get a lot worse...

CHAPTER 11

Twisted Fate... New Daughter?

Janix's room hours after the
meeting with Rústīcar

Setting the room up accordingly, I got little Nae to sleep in a little crib that I asked Steefas to find...—I'm not going to ask him how he found a perfectly good crib completely unattended— Ignoring the initials 'SB' on the railing, I checked the sturdiness and then asked Steefas to watch over her and to keep an eye on Bella who got the bed.

A few hours passed as I laid with Steefas, waiting until I couldn't wait any longer. Getting up for the door, I analyzed the room one more time before walking out. Closing the door I continued down the hallway, very aware of the eyes that were following me in the shadows. There was something sinister lurking about the palace and it was keeping a very close eye on me. All the way until I finally made it to the door, slipping in and away from the prying eyes that followed.

Andreas and Dehaas sat in a corner of the room talking quietly amongst themselves while a singular orb of angelic white light hovered above them. The orange glow of fire was in front of them, flickering in the shadows that were ever present. It was evident that what was happening in the fire was of immense importance as they appeared transfixed by the flame's intensity as it continued to play images throughout their conversation.

Walking up I saw in the flames, a teenager dressed in a cloak and armor, much like that of myself and Ailani. She wielded a saber in her right hand with a belt of throwing knives across her chest. She was quick and precise, cutting down the flame enemies with the skill and grace of a trained assassin. Her gauntlets looked to be thin but strong as they held against blows from other weapons that the blazing fighters wielded. Launching into the air with her blades poised and ready, she struck down the final enemy, whose own blade caught her hood. I looked at her in shock, as I realized that she bared remarkable resemblance to that of Ailani... this was her child... I was witnessing, a teenager Nae through the vision of fire.

"What the hell is going on here?" I finally asked, Andreas and Dehaas immediately snuffed out the fire, leaving only the angelic light above as they turned to me with grim faces.

"Janix, what you saw was your daughter," Dehaas stated confusing the hell out of me.

"What are you talking about, I have no children and that looked like Ailani," I reasoned to them. "The only child that Ailani has, is little Nae, and they won't even know the joys of growing together."

"NO! Janix," Andreas started strong before evening his voice back to normal. "that night you and Ailani finally consummated, Ailani was very much pregnant with your child. However, the Lord took it upon himself to take the child from y'all during the battle, it wasn't just her life that he saved, it was hers and the girl." He continued leaving me completely baffled. *What does this even mean, surely he's not saying what I think he's saying...* These thoughts rolled through my head as Dehaas continued.

"When our Father did this Janix, he wiped Ailani's memories of you and replaced them with Alex because he knew that you would need the mental fortitude to continue. After this, we took it upon ourselves to age and train her. You will also be closely working with your own daughter." Sitting there in both shock and deep thought, I couldn't help but be in denial... the Lord... he... he took a daughter from me? No... it couldn't be, this is just some hoax, right?

"Please tell me this is a bad joke?!??" I asked hopeful. Yet, when they didn't waver in their dark expressions, there was no helping the anger that began to bubble deep within my mental intrepidity, the anger that's been well suppressed in the deepest depths of my mind.

"This has to be a bad joke, right?!" I questioned again, my calm voice holding danger to it. "Janix, I assure you that this is no joke." Andreas replied to which I finally snapped.

"Well it freaking MUST BE!" I exclaimed. "OTH-ERWISE THAT WOULD MEAN *GOD* NOT ONLY TWISTED MY FORSAKEN LIFE, HE ALSO TOOK A DAUGHTER FROM ME. FOR TWO YEARS I DID-N'T EVEN KNOW SHE EXISTED... AND NOW YOU'RE TELLING ME THAT SHE'S ALIVE, ALREADY A WARRIOR!!!" I was livid right now, I felt the angelic and demonic power within me joining together, my black wings extending from my back and shadows around me closing in only to get pushed back by the angelic light which kept them at bay.

Dehaas looked at me unconcerned, merely yawning at my outburst as his arms remained crossed. It was evident that my supernaturally mixed aura began to intensify as small tendrils of yellow lightning flashed around my hands.

I discovered the lightning while pressed between a hard place and a very complicated decision involving the freeing of numerous prisoners who were taken by the An-gels a long time ago. Lets' just say that in its discovery, was the result of a lot of electrified angelic turkeys.

"Janix, calm yourself," Dehaas said just as bored as he looked. "We still have much to discuss and you'll get your chance to meet her soon." I didn't like it, but even in my rage, I understood that there was a bigger picture to this... but I would get answers and repayment for this transgression. Forcing the built up energies within me to mellow down, I retracted my wings but there was nothing to keep the aura from being noticeably large.

"What more could we possibly have to discuss." I asked in as civil of a tone I could. The tension in room was thick enough that one could almost cut through it.

"This threat, it is bigger than anything you've ever had to deal with."

"Well obviously, I got the picture when I watched it in the vision that Lucifer showed me."

Ignoring me he continued, "It's larger than you can imagine, this thing is a world ender, something that even our Father had a difficult time beating."

"Mind you," Andreas jumped in, "in the old age, our legions of angels were twice that, then our numbers were half that two years ago before the war. Now, we are but a fraction of the army that use to be. Still vast in comparison to that of a mortal army, but insignificantly small compared to that of what we face." He finished but that just left me more confused than anything else.

"So you're telling me that the situation is hopeless, what's the point of this then? Why shouldn't the world just abandon the thought of survival?"

They stared at me for a minute before Andreas snapped his fingers. The orb of light that was hovering over us descended, getting brighter and brighter until it began to grow and morph. It looked as if a star were being manipulated into that of a humanoid shape. Arms and legs formed themselves from the light until the form appeared to be in a kneeling position, the light that glowed dimmed slowly until caramel skin began to replace it, wavy dark brown hair solidified in a braid. When the light dimmed she stood, naked as a new born child, but with the look of a fierce warrior. She was only a young teenager but she was the spitting image of Ailani, just a lot younger, yet...

her eyes, instead of Ailani's electric blues that I could get lost forever in was deep reddish gold irises, the color of my eyes…

She seemed to regard me just as much as I did her.

"Hello, Father." Her voice was sharp and stern, not at all that of a girl who should be in her young teen years. Ripping a curtain down—Katrina can bill me later— I handed it to her. After she wrapped herself in it, I finally replied.

"Don't call me that." I stated. It was much too early for that bullshit. That is exactly what all of this is, complete and utter bullshit.

"Janix will be just fine until we get to know each other better."

She turned her head to Andreas before raising an eyebrow in a disturbing similarity to how I do. With another snap, there was a quick flash from under the curtain and when the girl let the it fall, she was dressed much like how she was in the fire. Clothed in tall black leather boots and skin tight pants that allowed her full movement and flexibility. She wore a fringed leather shirt and two gauntlets that appeared as black as obsidian with a saber strapped to her waist—*I'll need to request a special order from Katrina to assist me in smithing her new sword… again, I thought*— Sashed across her chest was a bandoleer of throwing knives that were easy to grab. Not bad… but I'll still have to test her tomorrow.

"Janix, allow me to introduce your daughter, Kailiana."

Once the introductions were out of the way, and the Angels passed on the information, I called for a servant to kindly show Kailiana to her chambers. Neither of us said much more as we were both extremely unsure of each other. Andreas and Dehaas left through a portal, I retired myself to my chambers, shedding my shirt and drifting into a restless sleep in the beautifully soft black fur of Steefas..

CHAPTER 12

Wrath of Old Lovers

The land was a chaotic wasteland... bodies of my friends littered the landscape, Angels, Demons, men, women and children all torn to shreds as the hulking mass of Cûrburõs walked, shaking the earth with every step that he took. The three headed hound leered down at me, hate and rage filling the eyes of every head that wanted nothing more than to squash me. However... Falling to all fours, the three heads looked at me, cackling with glee.

"**Child of mine enemy!**" It was the middle head that rasped, the sound of his voice like that of a thousand knives scraping against metal. The fear that filled me was overwhelming, yet, I was unable to run. I was unable to speak, all I could do was watch and pray to the All-father that I would be alright.

"**Yes, you're right to fear *us*, boy! If this wasn't a dream then *we* would take your head with *our* tail right now, feeding your corpse to the demons that were wise enough to join *our* side. Look around you Janix.**" I saw my friends and family surrounding me now, all brandishing weapons and standing in front of me. "**Your little armies are nothing!**" The left head bellowed before raking a hand across the field and slaughtering most of the villagers of Véchenti. I saw Aarönin, with a new and quite large white scar that ran down his left arm, he looked frail, aged beyond that of his usual appearance. He looked tired, saddened, he looked beyond himself as I watched as the tail of Cûrburõs whipped across. Taking his head clean off his shoulders.

"**Remember this boy,**" Stabbing its pointed tail through the separated head of Aarönin, he dangled it in front of my face. "**Your pitiful friends!**"

"**ARE NOTHING!**" The three heads spoke in unison, shaking the dream as I woke up sweating.

Sun light broke through the window over the bed that I just now realized was there. Bella and little Nae were still fast asleep, Steefas was still curled in the position that we went to sleep in. Calming my nerves, I stood, dawning a shirt and stepping out to the hallway. There is so much I have to think about and contend with. But there is only so much I can truly do... I don't want to lose my friends at all, it was clear that what I saw, was a vision of a potential future. It was also clear, that there was a demon following me again as the feeling of pure malice was hovering over my shoulders and I was unable to shake it. Whatever this is, I need to figure it out.

"All right! I know you're there!" I said drawing my dagger with my right hand. I've taken to keeping one on my belt as I no longer have Ailani's sword strapped to my hip.

That said, depending on what it was, I would like to just tell it off and be done with it. I really wasn't looking to kill in Katrina's palace...well, that was the plan until the lights dimmed, bugs of all kinds swarmed outside. Blocking out the sun from allowing light into the room. I was in a corridor with very little visibility, I was alone... it was just like that time in the forest. Just like that time before the battle when I was subdued by my old lover, and just like last time, melting out of the shadows, Zoe Hill was standing before me.

"Hello, little maggot." She said.

"Why are you here?" I questioned, she had no business being here, especially knowing what I would do to her now that I finally had her.

"Please," she began cockily. "Did you really think your girlfriend would be able to beat me?" She smirked "Maybe the old Zoe would have been killed by her..." laughing, she raised her hands, revealing her red leather one piece suit, with a perfect V parting between her breasts down to her belly button. "But, even you can see that I'm not the old Zoe!" She said blocking my blade with her own as I appeared faster than the blink of an eye, my blade barely an inch from her throat. "Maggot, now that's not very nice!" She said condescendingly. "And here I was wishing to converse with you." I attempted to punch her, which she shifted her head at the last second. My fist slammed straight into the stone wall, causing it to shudder from the amount of force I put into it.

"TALK!!! AFTER YOU ATTEMPTED TO MURDER ME IN THE FOREST!?!!" My blood mixed together, my wings extending from my back, my teeth slightly elongated into fangs that barely protruded from my lips. If I looked in a mirror, I was certain that my eyes were pitch black, like that of an abyss. I wouldn't let her live past this day.

Sighing, she looked at me, evaporating and reappearing behind me. "Look, as hard as it may be to accept, I don't want to fight you."

"Yeah, well I don't exactly see how you have a choice!" I was blind with rage, the world was red and all I could see was my target. The target I was about to gut, about to skewer, about to rip limb from limb. Who the hell does this girl think she is, how dare she show her face to me after what she did. I attacked again, my smaller blade cutting through her scimitar only to get blown back by a mysterious unforeseen blast of energy. The wind was knocked out of me, leaving me panting on the ground from the hidden blow, I wasn't hurt, but at the same time it was like I just went toe to toe with Michael again...

"JANIX! YOU WILL NOT HARM HER!" The voice of Rústicar cut through the walls. "While here, she is under my protection as well as the protection of other beings, YOU will not touch her." The shock I felt mutated into an outburst of pure rage.

"How can you take this from me!!! After the amount of problems this woman has caused!" I yelled at the ceiling before taking a deep breath to calm myself. Looking at the form of Zoe, I let out a long and deep sigh… revert-ing back to my human appearance.

"Whatever you have to say, 'urry up. I want this interaction as brief as possible." I stated with a great deal of irritation in my voice. In reality, now that my storm of anger was subsiding, I wouldn't be able to keep up my angry or even stoic face for long.

Staring at me with a look of disgust and anger, she finally sighed before casting her gaze downward.

"I've come to the conclusion that in order for me to survive, it would be in my best interest to ally myself with your growing legion."

"And why? Pray tell, why would we ever let you join us?" She tried to kill me two years ago, tried to sabotage our unification of species. Now, she wants to join me? Something wasn't right, what could her motive be? I was interrupted from my thoughts when she let out an exaggerated sigh.

"Overthinking everything as usual aren't you?" She said with a slight smirk before looking up at me. My mind had to be playing tricks on me, because for all of two seconds I could have sworn I saw the old Zoe again. Her mischievous nature shining through her cold looks, then she spoke again. "I always did find that cute about you…" in that statement, the deepest part of me that wanted her to be the girl I use to know tried to come out. My solid and stoic posture wavering, her voice was calm, smooth and beautiful… exactly like the Zoe I knew in the past. Bringing myself out of it, I couldn't help but chuckle at that idea before solidifying my pissed off look again.

"Cut the bullshit!" I exclaimed, "Quit talking like you want my blessing to join our side, No!" She was trying to retort with something, but I held up my hand, silencing her. "I would never accept you to join me, as a servant to no one, I can afford to make that kind of decision." Turning to walk away, "However, I can't make that decision as one man, not in the name of everyone who needs to live. Stay out of my way, I'm sure that Rústícar will find you a place in our ranks." Walking away from her, I heard her sigh and then... her presence dissipated into the shadows, leaving me alone once more.

"Master?" Steefas asked walking up to me.

"What do you need?"

"Just... that was her, wasn't it?"

"Yeah, after two years, she's finally shown herself. Then just as I'm about to finish what she started, I'm not even allowed the simplest form of revenge."

"Well I can't say that I blame you or your feelings Janix." Andreas' voice sounded as he morphed from the shadows, "but as Rústícar stated, she is under the protection of himself and a number of other beings. Now, follow me, it is time that we talk about your training." Turning, Andreas opened a portal to what I assume will be the training area that we will utilize.

"Steefas, I need you to look after little Nae, also I need you to keep that knight of hell in check. Will you be ok with that?"

"Not a problem," Steefas replied before a mischievous smirk appeared. "Nix."

I scowled at him but wasn't able to retort as Andreas beckoned me through the portal to the other side.. reviewing once again... a massive mountain that I just had a feeling that I would have to climb in order to properly train... not exactly what I wanted to do as I remembered what happened with the shapeshifter and Ailani...

Speaking of Ailani, standing one hundred yards away from where we exited the portal, spell after spell of pure destruction, was Ailani in glistening golden armor. Arcs of magic flew from her hands and saber in a beautiful display of swordsmanship and marital arts. Golems rose around her, acting as her current challengers and numbering in the hundreds. Seeing so many surrounding her and no one else helping her out I couldn't keep my comment quiet.

"Andreas, isn't that a bit much… I have no doubts about her skill having trained her myself but…" I was about to continue until the Roving angel held up a hand silencing me. Putting a finger to his lips, he pointed to her.

She stood confident and unwavering, perfect in stance with each leg bent lightly, saber poised in her right hand, the obsidian black blade pointed downward as she brought her hand up to her face. She appeared to be saying something that I couldn't distinguish as the legions began to charge. However, it was too late for the Golems, as the first one reached her getting cut down by Ailani's saber in a simple slash before raising her sword upward as if she were a conductor. The sky swirled about her and a tendril of lightning flashed, impacting the saber which appeared to be absorbing the energy before the electricity was swirling around the blade. In a mighty yell she then thrust the blade into the earth.

Everything appeared to happen in slow motion. The energy wave blew her opponents back, then the energy that was stored within the blade lashed out in all directions. As if the force of the lighting strike was being harnessed in the same ferocity cutting down the clay warriors in mighty explosions. Arcs of lightning branching out from the main tendrils, sending the electricity in other directions before getting absorbed by the earth.

Ailani stood as the last of the clay warriors disintegrated into the earth. Only to turn and see me, it was then… that I knew I was screwed.

CHAPTER 13

Training and a Shark thing?

Everything was frozen in time, the wind nonexistent as she strode up to us. My breath seizing upon laying my eyes on her, Ailani, walking with purpose and a stoic expression. Golden armor gleaming like that of a goddess born of the sun. However, it looked heavy and bulky, not at all complimenting her style that I knew she had mastered as well as the fact that she seemed to rely purely on the knowledge that her powers would protect her... all in all, she seems to have completely thrown away my training that I had instilled in her so long ago.

I was pissed... but that anger turned to shock as she walked up, back handing me with such force that it jarred my mind to its core.

"Don't look at me like that Janix!" She exclaimed indignantly. "You lost that claim long ago when you abandoned me to be the wife of **Alex**." Her once stoic gaze now chalked full with anger. Ailani's eyes flashed silver with power as she sent a fiery blue palm into my chest creating a shock wave and sending me into a hillside. This power was at least twice that of what she had before and... something told me that she was still holding back. That blast knocked the wind out of me as I coughed up a little blood.

"In the dog house now aren't you Janix?" Came the bemused voice of Kailiana, a massive smirk upon her face. I would have retorted had I not been forced to draw my dagger to parry a rather slow slash from Ailani.

"Don't take your eyes off of me you presumptuous pile of excrement." Her blade fell slower but still full of power. So much so that I couldn't help but comment.

"So the student has forsaken her teachings of speed and precision to become a sluggish brute of force and misguided quarrel?" I finished, blocking a pathetically weak stab she had aimed at my midsection. "Not only this, but I see you have discarded the equipment of agility that better suits your body ty…" I was unable to finish as a bolt of lighting was sent at me. Dodging, a massive crater appeared where I had been standing just seconds ago. She's no longer up to par with me on swordsmanship, but even I'd feel the repercussions of a blast like that… held back or not.

"Shut up, who are you to lecture me…" Her silver eyes were solid, no whites shown at all. "after two years of neglecting I was even alive…" She took a step and all around, I could feel the elements bending to her electrical attacks. "after two years of abandoning me…" in a flurry of fast body motions, much like that of the old martial arts known as Tai chi, balls of red and blue energy began to swirl around her as a purple aura engulfed her being. An amazing and beautiful display… if it wasn't for the fact it was directed at me… "After waiting till I was pregnant and still not telling me the truth." I watched as a single tear fell from her eye, "You think you have a right to tell me anything about what I do anymore!?!" Bringing the two colors together, they merged as one creating a fluorescent color scheme of ever changing lighting. Then in the same motion, she pulled her hands apart, before meeting her left bicep with her right hand and directing two fingers with her left towards me. Sending a massive assault of energy.

Dropping my arms, I closed my eyes in acceptance. If this is what it took for her to heal, then so be it… I waited, and waited, for the blast that never impacted. But even with my eyes closed I could feel the force of the attack that was diverted just meters ahead of me and the winds wiped and swirled all around. Opening my eyes, I was being protected by not only Andreas, but Dehaas as well who both formed an 'X' with their holy blades combined. I looked at their feet to see the powerful attack had been redirected and cut down the middle. Two molten craters passed on each side as we were in the center of a massive 'V'. The roving angels' blades red hot with the heat of Ailani's attack.

"We may have made a mistake Dehaas... allowing her memories to come back all at once..." Andreas commented.

"You think!" Dehaas snapped back. "How was I supposed to know she'd react this bad! But at least we know we have more than one potential cannon." Dehaas finished while looking back at me with a smirk. Both Angels dropping their guard as Bella stepped through a portal with-straining Ailani.

"I think we need to calm this one before she at-tempts to kill Janix again." Walking up to her, Andreas took his middle and ring finger touching her forehead making her collapse into Bella's arms and getting dragged into a portal.

"Now!" Exclaimed Dehaas, "It is time for yours and Kailiana's training to begin." I glowered at him.

"Do I really need to train with *him?*" Gripped a rather bored looking Kailiana. Raising my eyebrows at the blatant disrespect, I looked to Andreas who simply nodded his head.

"Think you know how to use that blade girl?" I asked her. This was going to happen sooner or later, and now wasn't the time to question the two angels about Ailani... no matter how much it pained me.

"Girl!?" She exclaimed. "I'll have you know that I'm the best agent that's been produced by lords Dehaas and Andreas."

"Really?" I asked raising an eyebrow at said angels who just shrugged sheepishly. Time to take this pup down a peg or two.

"Then beating me should prove easy for you. DRAW YOUR WEAPON." I wasn't going to draw my blade for this, I want to see her reactions and speed. I need to know her baseline.

"Well? Aren't you going to at least draw that knife on your belt?" She asked slightly confused at my challenge but lack of weapon. Smirking, I asked Andreas to hold my Machete and dagger, having left my throwing knives and hidden blades in the room.

"Don't worry about me." I tightened the modified bracers I requested Katrina to supply me with before we left. "I'll take your saber when you're through with it." I took a strong mountainous stance. My left hand out and flexed, three fingers straight and elongated while my pointer and thumb were bent. My left arm bent at a thirty degree angle. Then my right hand, poised at my midsection, ready to deal out the finishing blow.

"If you say so, don't blame me when you're cut to hell, *FATHER!*" With that, she launched her attack off furious swipes and stabs with her saber. Her aim was true, as I was forced to utilize my gauntlets thus deflecting her at-tacks. All in all, she wasn't bad... for an amateur. Her leg work was good, but still needs work, I would have tripped her up five moves ago, not to mention that she was using a moderately flashy tactic. One that would have been near unnoticeable had I not been trained and honed for this kind of fighting with Ailani. She still moved and reacted with the speed and grace of a young godling—and being honest, she basically is— but she still had much to learn... especially about underestimating her opponents.

Having seen enough, I blocked a swipe with my left arm, stepping into her guard before grabbing her belt with my right rolling her over my shoulders causing her to drop the saber which I scooped up and held at her exposed throat.

"You have much to learn young one. You project your moves leaving you seconds too late to react to a proper attack, your instinct was to let go of your sword instead of attempting to utilize your left arm to grab your sword an attack me, you toss it away." I stated all of this offering her a hand to which she knocked away before standing herself. Her head was down cast and full of shame at having been bested like the child she was.

"Yeah, well…" she tried to begin but stopped talking as the words got lost in her thoughts.

"Don't worry Kailiana!" I said laughing before un-sheathing my own blade. "Your mother and I use to duel all the time back when we were fighting together. Shit, she was the greatest fighter with a saber that I've ever had the pleasure of knowing…" as I finished this, my mind trailed off to distant memories. That seemed to be clouding my mind today as well as the fact that we really don't have a lot of time to be worrying about trivial tasks with a being like Cûrburõs out there about to bring the beginning of the dark-ages.

I was brought out of my thoughts by a strong scoff and followed by "I have no mother, Janix, I was just a creation of the lord and your seed was used to assist the creation of myself." I looked to the angels once again, I couldn't understand how the hell my own blood could be so… reclusive to that of everyone else around her… especially one as young as her… that is until I realized…

"Kailiana… how old are you, technically."

"Ask them." She gestured to Dehaas and Andreas who just watched us with interest.

"Officially?" Dehaas asked.

"Or bodily?" Andreas also asked.

"Freaking both for lords sake!" I exclaimed at them both. Even Kailiana couldn't help but crack a grin at the idiocy of the questions as they knew perfectly well what I was asking.

"Well, officially, she is just shy of being three-years old, her birthday coming up on July third." Dehaas started. I nodded my head with interest, that will be cutting it close, but that will be the perfect day for me to gift her the items… assuming that

Katrina is willing to take up the forge once again… given her queenly duties, she will no doubt be busy.

"Bodily however, she is 15 but with the real birth day coming up, she will be 16." Andreas finished.

'*Perfect!*' I thought, giving the two turkeys a nod of appreciation. I was turning my attention back to Ana,— Kailiana's nick name I'm going to give her, as Kailiana is kind of a mouthful…— when suddenly a new voice jumped in.

"Why are you so interested Janix?" A man clad in leather bracers and a steel chest plate walked up to us, a massive broadsword strapped to his back. Three large scars passed from his left ear and rounded down to his throat where a chunk of flesh appeared to be missing. It was a wonder that he was even alive… seeing that he had survived a wound like that.

"Um… forgive me for answering a question… with another, but who are you?"

"Oh! Uncle Axilious." Ana exclaimed, much to my confusion.

"Uncle?" I asked.

"My apologies young Janix, I'm a member of your old village… back in Kanixwa. I'm sure that you don't…" he wasn't able to finish thought as I suddenly remembered.

"Cousin Leo! Is that really you?" I asked, utilizing his older nick name as it appeared that his new front was Axilious.

"So you do remember me then!" He laughed boisterously. "To think, you left just to be a grunt with your sis-ter, and now look at you! You're a bloody General and a… Janix… what's with the eyes?" I was so happy that I didn't realize I had been allowing my demonic energy to build making my eyes black and on a whim, the angelic and de-monic energies were ready to merge together.

"Sorry, just a little excited." I stated before pushing my energies back down, subduing them. "A lot has happened since we were kids. What brings you to this part of the world... and here no less?"

He was about to answer when suddenly the earth shook violently, a crack in the center of the training area appeared as molten rock seeped up with that of a massive beast. It glowered at us as it rose to its true height of 25 feet.

All of us were frozen, as the beast reared its massive shark like head to the sky releasing a terrible scream. I didn't know what the hell it was, but I knew one thing... Lucifer and I needed to have a talk about this three headed hound if some creature like this was coming to our realm.

CHAPTER 14

A New Ally?

LOOK OUT!!!" I yelled to Kailiana who dodged a swipe of the lizard shark creatures tail. On the other side of the beast Axilious himself drew his impressively large sword charging the beast head on. The creature attempted to snap its jaws at him only to get a swipe to the lower jaw. Sadly, the attack was in vain as the sword merely bounce off of its skin, much like that Steefas' fur when facing normal weapons. I extended my wings, joining the roving angels in flight. The angels themselves had sheathed their silver sabers and harnessed the power spears created from the very essence of light. One after the other, spears sailed right at its massive head, exploding and illuminating the sky in a spectacle of lights and heavenly flame. It did no noticeable damage.

"EVERYONE GET CLEAR! I'M UNLEASHING THE CURSE OF JAXHUR!" I yelled out before flying higher above the dreaded creature.

"Nix ür lan dùr mó…" I began, holding my Ma-chete out and exposing the blade to the cosmos. "… ithén duc nâr ét sintre…" fire ignited along the blade of Shinxi-tar— A fitting name I gave the black Machete of matter, loosely translated from the angelic language too, **The Soulless Sword**— "nöc tun discrimitar tyn JAXHUR!!!" Sweat dripped from my brow as my energy was being sapped. This is attack would work, it had too. My willpower was only strong enough for this one attack before I would be out of commission for the rest of the day and into the night. With the final word uttered from the incantation, tendrils of hell fire and light flew from my blade. Shinxitar felt heavier in my hands as I began my dive towards the unholy creature of hell. I didn't necessarily have to kill it, I just needed the blade to touch it for the curse to take effect. This is exactly what happened, as I blew past it, my blade pulling from the drag as the skin still wasn't penetrated by Shinxitar.

There was a massive flash, and wind was sucked in before being expunged outwardly casing a mushroom cloud to rise around the area. Everything within a hundred meter radius was blown to hell, the curse of Jaxhur taking effect as the landscape was mutilated, skeletal black hands gripping anything and everything within reach, flailing like a new creature was attempting to pull itself from the earth. However, it's really terraforming everything underfoot of the bizarre creature, causing the massive shark head to release a blood curdling and piercing noise indescribable to a mortals perspective. A wailing eruption of pain, equivalent to that of millions of souls perishing in the scorching inferno of hell fire, as if hell itself were projecting the cries of the eternally damned. The creature was then dragged into the deep chasm, in a final shudder, the ground closed itself... the group had been successful, they were victorious.

Janix landed with the others as they all gathered together, the three supernatural being exhausted from spiritual and magical exertion. Kailiana and Leo also exhausted from dodging the barrage of random attacks as they were just as ineffective as Janix was.

Taking a deep breath, Kailiana exclaimed "Janix! What the hell was that?"

"I don't know..." replied the tired half breed as he looked back to his cousin Leo.

"So, welcome to this side of the world, what brings you here… also, how do you know Kailiana?" Simple questions from me, probably far simpler than they should have been. However after the amount of hell I've endured during the last… decade, I was more than pissed off al-ready with fate for forging the current path I'm on. Not to mention that Leo's from my home village.

"I could ask you the same thing cousin, I'm her as Kailiana's guardian." He replied looking to the angels. Raising an eyebrow, I also looked to the angels who held up their arms in surrender.

"Look, as much as we trust that you will be able to bring down Cûrburõs… it would make us in the silver city feel bet… " this was as far as Dehaas was able to get before the ground exploded from under our feet sending all of us flying seventy feet into the air. I caught Kailiana who looked down bashfully as I held her in my arms.

"You alright?" I asked sincerely concerned, her body doesn't have the durability that we supernatural beings obtain upon transformation, so I needed to make sure that she was ok.

"I'm fine, just… can you put me down now please." I nodded my head before locating a safe place. I couldn't believe my eyes, that curse was suppose to send that creature on a one-way trip to hell itself. How the fuck was it unaffected by its effects.

Landing away from the battle zone, I looked at my daughter, "Kailiana, you need to run!"

"Run?!" She protested indignantly once I set her down.

"YES! Look, there is nothing that you or Leo will be able to do. That was my best attack against a creature like this." I explained. I needed her to get it through her head that I needed her gone, I can't beat this creature… whatever the hell it is, and we were all already tired as Leo ran up to us.

"Cousin! What's the plan?" He asked taking in the situation.

I couldn't help but smirk at the old phrase he used to say when were kids.

"Things never change do they? Once again I have to come up with the plan." I chuckled at long forgotten memories that surfaced before grasping his hand, "Well, the plan is that you're going to take Kailiana and get out of here." I state to his shocked expression before looking at my daughter.

"Janix!?" She exclaimed confused as I continued to talk to Leo while looking at her. My expression firm and strong. The complete opposite of how I felt about this situation.

"Make sure that y'all are getting away from here, do not interfere, as y'all will only get in the way. Watch over her Leo." Releasing his arm, I looked at the beast once again, drawing Shinxitar. I could tell that he wanted to argue, hoping that there was another way, but even he under-stood that this was something only I could do with Dehaas and Andreas. I knew he accepted that... however, what he said next froze me in place.

"Godspeed Nôktor." My eyes widened in shock, I looked back for only a second to see the two of them running away from the area. To my left, the land exploded showering me in dirt after Dehaas impacts the ground, his right wing bent at an unusual angle and Andreas was grabbed in the beasts vice like grip. With sheer angelic strength, he attempted to fight off the hand, slightly making the hand budge until the creature held him by a leg and arm, tearing both off with ease. Andreas released a scream of agony as his mutilated body was dropped to the ground. Light seeping out of his wounds.

The creature bared down on me, there was nothing I could do. I was about to face my maker, and I had yet to do anything to assist in the survival against Cûrburõs. I, Janix, was a failure.

Analyzing the beast, I finally had enough of this waiting, if I was to die, I would die with the dignity of a warrior.

"COME ON!!!" I taunted.

"You want me, then let's GO!!!" I exclaimed before charging the jaws of death which suddenly opened at mul-tiple angles making the head look like a flower with jagged teeth on each flap.

Yet... as I charged, the earth once again began to quake stopping both of us in our tacks. "Great!!! Now what!!!" I exclaimed to no one in particular.

A fissure in the earth opened as blaring horns sounded. The horns of hell sounding as a flaming chariot pulled by skeletal stallions erupted into the world. Controlling the reigns, was a massive man adorned in skeletal arm and shin guards, his chest protected by bronze and a scull helm over his head. The warrior drew a sword that appeared very familiar, but at this distance he couldn't be sure... he prayed to the gods of Earth that he was wrong. Riding around the monstrosity, the large Knight of hell jumped off of the chariot and charged at full speed towards the beast.

'Great, this joker is about to get himself killed before he can even do anything.' I thought before I was proven wrong. The warrior lobbed off the beasts right hand in a single swipe. He continued without fear, releasing a guttural war cry of rage as he slashed at the beast's legs casing it to fall to its knees. Then in a quick motion, took the shark head clean off. Just like that, the fight was over, as if fighting this creature was like fighting a child. Who is this warrior? Who is this Knight of Hell that has come to our rescue? More importantly, what is it that he wants?

Whipping the blood from his blade, the warrior stood, now that I could see more clearly, I saw that a red cape with a black goat head draped over his shoulders. Re-moving the sabertooth skull that he wore as a helm, he stood approaching us. Andreas was still healing his severed arm and leg, then Dehaas was still milking a broken wing unconscious. I was the only line of defense, its quite possible... that I have just been introduced to someone far worse than that creature we were unable to defeat. That is... until the warrior stopped right in front of me, upon further examination, he was just a bit taller than me, about six feet six point six inches... 666, long brown hair brushed over to the right side of his face, and blood red eyes that held an odd look of mirth to them. He looked the part of a demon, but the casual and laid back feeling that radiated off of him was unnerving. It got even weirder when he extended his arm for a handshake, I was adamant, but took it cautiously, eyeing the blade that I now confirmed the identity of.

"Name's RÿJunìc, right hand to the Lord of Sin, Military adviser to Lord Lucifer, General to the army of Satan, Commander to the legions known as the Knights of Hell... at-least what's left of them."

CHAPTER 15

Loss of a Cousin

To say that I was in shock would be a gross understatement. Even in the upper world, most of the living beings of the planet have heard of this leader. He is famous as the strongest of the Knights of Hell, not only this, but he is now topside and breathing the fresh air of the land. Lu-cifer and I seriously need to talk about what the Hell is go-ing on around here.

"RÿJunìc, up here with the living and breathing…" I whispered as our hands were still clasped.

"Janix of…"

"…the 6ᵗʰ Angelic division— Hells destruction — leader to the five greatest heroes of the Reckoning war, soul surviver of a lost angelic cause, hell bound final agent to the Lord, and Bane of Michael." RÿJunic finished throwing me into a bigger stupor at the fact he, of all creations, knew my titles. He tightened his grip on my hand. His expression changing from amused to stoic and his voice held a tone of anger and irritation. We stared each other down, eyes locked and neither backing down.

"You, Lord Janix, are one pain in the ass for my subordinates." He stated chuckling.

"Yo… you know me?" He stopped chuckling and just looked at me with shock.

"KNOW YOU!!! SATANS HORNS!!! Your famous in the underworld. Not only this, but I recall you being the reason that we lost my best Knight who I was hoping would take my place one day. Hell, if memory serves, she almost recked your shit!" He continued laughing slapping me on the shoulders good naturally. Can this really be the Right hand of Lucifer? This… red eyed tall and chill dude? Not only that, but he couldn't be talking about who I think… however, she is the only one that I've fought be-fore. Maybe it is time that Bella and I had a talk.

I would have contemplated this for a longer period of time had it not been for the fact that Dehaas released a groan of pain.

"Damn it!" I exclaimed.

"Steefas? Can you hear me?"

'Yes master, is everything well? The Knight returned with a very… ill looking form of your old mate.'

"We need a portal here now, Andreas and Dehaas are badly injured, and we need to get everyone else back to the palace. Also, tell Bella that we need to talk." I didn't have to wait long as Steefas understood the tone in my thoughts within moments, a portal was opened by Lucifer who ushered all of us in before asking a random hell hound to find Kailiana and Leo to bring them back as well. All in all, it was utter chaos.

ARRIVING IN KATRINAS THROWN ROOM

Upon arriving back in the Palace of Katrina, Lucifer and RÿJunìc assisted in carrying the angels to the medical room. Where they'd have the chance to recharge their angelic prowess and properly heal. I was relatively fine if not a little battered and disoriented, I was also covered in sweat and dirt but refused to leave until the return of my cousin and daughter. I may not approve of how she was aged, or the fact that God messed with my life in a bigger way than should have been possible. I would still act as a guardian to her… it didn't matter though, I made it clear that our relationship is strictly would be strictly master and apprentice. A choice I know that I will never regret, the pain of losing those in the living realm is too much already.

I will not deal with the bullshit of life herself... again. My thoughts continued down this dark path as I just couldn't shake how amazing it is that so many emotions can run through the mind of one individual. How much hate, passion, pain, hid-den suffering can be suffocated. But every one has a breaking point that will all ways snap if pushed hard enough to the right side. It is for this reason the beings of this known world join various allegiances. But... What about the ones who can't cope with the pain. So many, children, teenagers, adults, veterans, hell... even elderly men and women kill themselves in so many gruesome ways just too end the suffering. I would have continued my quickly dwindling thoughts until the voice of RÿJunìc pierced through my thought process and breaking me out of my stupor.

"Your going to hurt yourself thinking so hard, Lord Janix."

"Sir RÿJunìc!?"

"Tell me son, what ails thee." He said pulling a tankard out of a bag he seemed to be carrying.

"Nothing of great importance." I lied. He laughed heartily.

"You should know better than to attempt lying to me Lord Janix." Smirking, I couldn't help but get amused by the oddity of Lucifer's General being so... brotherly...

"Let me ask you something Sir, where does the Lord come from? Why do you of all demonic creatures call me a lord."

He leaned on a pillar as I started walking towards him.

"Lord Janix?" He said again before looking down as if in deep contemplation. "The reason is simple, my trusted Lt. of the Knights spoke highly of your skill. She praised you as her equal. She told us of the warrior that nearly took her life but sent her away." As he spoke, my mind drifted back to the time of the reckoning war, when I came face to face with her for the first time.

"Bella never gave up much details, only that be-cause of you, she had a new appreciation for the aspect of life that we Knights of Hell usually don't get the opportunity to earn." I thought back to what she said to me when we saw each other in the room of Rústīcar, *"Well, if it's any consolation, I'm glad I didn't kill you."*

"Your saying... that by me sparing her life all that time ago..."

"You unknowingly created a rather weird situation where we Knights of Hell are willing to assist in the battle against a great evil... though, I wish the evil wasn't that damn dog..." RÿJunìc once again looked down, as if he were remembering a terrible memory.

"She never said anything..." I was dumbfounded by this revelation, yet RÿJunìc laughed before saying, "No, she wouldn't have I guess. That not her style. But she is the reason that even we Knights are willing to work with you."

"You... you know what it is we fight don't you?" He was unable to respond as a portal opened up. Kailiana and Axilious ran through with one of the Hellhounds that were tasked with searching for them...

"Please help us!!!" Kailiana screamed out as Axil-ious' sword clattered way from him. Then Axilious himself fell, convulsing on the ground foaming at the mouth. Kail-iana instantly rushed to him, cradling his head and begging for help. It was clear though, my cousin was dying and Kailiana was distraught with fear merging with anger.

Looking at each-other, RÿJunìc and I ran to help them. Upon seeing the state of Axilious for myself, I froze. He was in bad shape, a large bolt was sticking out of his right shoulder blade, the tip protruding out the front of his leather breast guard. Two more in his left leg and a dagger that looked as if it just missed his spinal cord by a fraction of an inch which would have paralyzed him. Blood leaked from his wounds creating a pool of blood on the floor. Kailiana getting dirtied with the blood of my cousin as he was gasping for air. Bits of his lung splayed on the triangular tip, mixing with a purple liquid, *poison.* His breathing was ragged, it was like he was experiencing a seizure.

Slowly, his eyes began to shut as he gasped his final breaths, attempting to tell Kailiana that everything would be ok.

"No... please God, no..." Kailiana whimpered, her tears falling from her face as we all watched my cousin ex-hale his last breath.

"Janix, please save him." She begged as all I could do was stand there in shock. "Save him, I can't lose my uncle." She said holding him closer as she wailed in emotional agony. "I..." she sniffled, "I can't lose the only family that I have."

"Damn it!!!" I exclaimed, biting my tongue. I closed my eyes turning away as years of memories sur-faced, I just had my cousin back, and now... he was taken... he was taken by someone that would rue the day that they ever touched my family. I walked up to Kailiana, gently pulling her away from my cousin. She stopped for only a second to look at me, our eyes meeting and only for an instant. Anger flashed before getting replaced by sadness. She latched onto me, burying her head into my chest. Now was not the time to go after them, I needed to comfort her in what I could... there will be time for revenge later.

Sensing my feelings, Steefas slowly emerged out of the shadows, no words needed to be exchanged as we both knew each other well enough to figure out what I had in mind and so, he soundless walked up to Axilious. Gripping the dagger in his jaws before pulling it out. Leaning down, he took in the scent before charging into the shadows once more. He understood that I would expecting a full report once he returned. But now was not the time, hugging Kailiana as I forced myself to withhold the rage I've suppressed these past few years. From the shadows I witnessed Egnachi appear only to let shadows envelop Axilious before vanishing. A conversation I'd have to have with Steefas later.

Katrina finally arrived after hearing all the commotion and her servants swarmed the room, armed guards sur-rounded the portal that was still open but slowly closing. RÿJunìc stood a respectful distance away. All in all, this was a shitty day.

CHAPTER 16

Darker Side of a Warrior

Hours passed, as I awaited the return of Steefas, with news of who it was that murdered my cousin in cold blood. After walking Kailiana back to her room, I left, al-lowing her the courtesy to grieve by herself. I myself on the other hand had a job at hand and revenge to plot. Giving Katrina a run down of what's happening, she put the entire palace on high alert as that training ground was never sup-posed to be a threat. Nor was there supposed to be hostile agents or civilians in the area that would lead to this.

"Janix... there is one more thing that I need to tell you."

With a sideways glare at a random pillar I asked with anger "What is it?" It was here that she told me everything about what happened in Véchenti. What happened to its people, and what happened to my poor apprentice.

"Janix, I know what it is you plan to do. Give them hell, and you don't have to take this as an order, but I recommend that you leave no survivors." She finished with great sadness. I simply nodded to her before walking away.

Once the debriefing was complete, I went back to my room only to be greeted by an obnoxiously chipper Bel-la who was playing with little Nae and teaching her how to organize various blades according to their length and purpose.

"How's it going *Nix*?" She asked bemused.

"Not now!" I replied sharply as I pulled my gear out of the storage locker directly across from the bed.

"Janix… your eyes…" she started before I silenced her with a sharp.

"I know!" And quicker "LEAVE ME BE." Opening the storage wrapping which held my gear, I strapped my belt of throwing knives across my chest as well as equip-ping my bow and arrows.

"Nix, look at me!" She made the mistake of at-tempting to grab my right shoulder as I reacted accordingly. Grabbing her hand with my left, fingers wrapping around it and twisting while drawing my blade pressing it to her throat. I did it without even thinking, I was so blind that I nearly pressed the blade harder until she let out an oddly quiet.

"Janix… please." blinking, I suddenly realized what I was doing before re-sheathing my blade and going back to what I was boing.

"I will explain later… Bella." I said before opening the door to the face of Steefas. The look in his eyes told me everything that he needed to. He found them, he knew their numbers, and he was ready to help me end them. "Take care of Nae, I'll be back… probably." With that I left clos-ing the door and jumping on Steefas back. "Take me to them."

"Master… before we…"

"**NOW!!!**" Understanding the message, he leaped into a shadow delivering us in the very center of a village that appeared quite quaint to that of Véchenti. There were kids running around and women doing some chores before noticing me. When I was finally noticed, the women had all the children go inside and locked the doors. With my advanced hearing I could hear all the locking mechanisms activate before only a barren looking street was before me. Looking around, it looked like a nice little plot of earth that had the potential of growing into a very successful city… should nothing catastrophic happen. The homes looked to be built of clay and stone, outside every home were flowers, bushes that complimented the small yards as a few older citizens stood outside staring at me. A few curious men stepped out when all the women left the area. One of them walked up to me with a pensive yet friendly look, "Excuse me sir, is there anything that we can help you wit..." I slit his throat without hesitation, he fell to the ground as I knelt, wiping my blade clean with his soiled clothes. The rest of the men suddenly ran inside, most com-ing back out with a weapon. Three arrows were shot at me and three arrows were cut from mid air, falling split in two and now harmless.

"Citizens of this shitty village! I am Janix. Hours ago my cousin was murdered in cold blood. I am here for one thing and one thing only, send me the ones involved in his murder." Six men walked out into the village center to meet him.

"Who the fuck do you thi..." I flicked my wrist, sending a knife into his throat silencing his pointless talk as he choked on his own blood.

"That's strike one, I don't give a fuck who the hell I need to kill, but any of you get in my way, *we* will kill this entire village." Steefas released a resonating growl that made all of the men shudder in sudden fear.

"That, you little piss ant, would be us." Three burly figures stepped away from one of the houses, all of them brandishing shields with a long sword or a battle ax.

"That's right. We're assuming you're a friend of that little asshole who tried to make off with that lass." One of the men stated.

"You should bring her back, we'd love to introduce her to three rods worthy of taking her virtue." Another stated. It was all I could do to keep from lashing out right then and there.

"Tell me, what are your names." It really didn't matter, I was going to kill them regardless of what they said.

"What's it matter, you're about to be slaughtered." The biggest one in the middle stated drawing his blade as the other men of the village came out to back them. My face down cast, I could feel the wind in the air, smell the order of the village, hear the creaking of the wooden porches that strained against the weight of some villagers. Then something strange happened, it was like a drum in my ears.

Thudunk… thudunk… thudunk…

Odd… that it is these spineless ingrates that seem to have steady heart beats. Clearly… they have never been faced with total annihilation. Still, I owe them one chance…

"I'll make you deal, either of you land ONE scratch on me, I will leave this village."

"You really think that you stand a chance against either of us."

"I know it, now all three of you, bring it." I spat on the ground showing my defiance as I was done talking. The first one came at me with a slash, which I side stepped and kicked him in the arse sending him into a pile of horse excrement. The other two came at me with a better strategy, they worked as one, they were a good team. Steefas just stayed behind watching with little interest as he was pestering me to just kill them. After fifteen attempts to even cut me I was finally done. The men were breathing heavily. Sighing, I just couldn't understand how this happened. But they will not get away.

"Steefas, no one leaves this shit hole… *ALIVE.*" Steefas nodded as he tensed his body, their minds were merged as one, they saw nothing but red, through each other's eyes, they understood what was happening, the two men that were behind the houses looking at us from there hiding place. I didn't know what was happening, but it was fine as Steefas released a howl so loud and powerful that it shook the land. Even from the center, I saw fire erupt in a ring and his children on the sides waiting for anyone. Tonight they would feed, tonight they embrace their baser instincts, tonight... I would embraced my baser instinct.

I didn't move fast, I walked casually towards them as the middle man attempted to raise his blade one last time. With a solid punch, my fist made contact with his chest, the crunch of his ribs breaking sounded with multiple pops and my hand pushed right through his spinal cord. My hand gripping his heart that still beat rapidly. He shuddered as his body went into shock screamed in pain as I crushed his heart. His blood splaying all over his two friends who were still alive. Ripping my hand out of his lifeless form I continued as the villagers attempted to swarmed me.

I sent three blades into the first group, making them fall lifeless and when I drew Shinxitar, I lobbed the head clean off of another villager. Before I knew it, the village reeked of blood. The smell would have been unnerving were I not so accustomed to it. The sight so ghastly were I not attuned to it. I was covered in gore as I was blood was literally dripping off of me. Mutilated corpses littered the ground, intestines of one that survived trailed behind a young boy that attempted to get out a window, he was crying for his mother as I silenced him with quick a decapitation. Then I moved on to his brother, I stabbed my blade through the child's chest causing him to scream in pain when I twisted my blade. The mother attempted to fend me off only to get back handed into the nearest wall creating a hole but leaving her limbs in the room. This village, its in-habitants, all were slaughtered as I went into each home. Everyone, every life I took just made me angrier and angrier. Man, woman, and child, none were safe from my wrath as I continued. The little village of forty dwindled into thirty, then twenty, until I was finally on the last two living souls. I sliced the arms off of a woman that was begging for her life. But I was too blind to listen, it didn't matter though, I was never meant to reach salvation anyway, Lucifer can punish me all he wants when I die. But for now, my revenge will not be sated until this village is wiped off the map. I kicked down the door to the last house, it held the third and final man that claimed to be a participant in my cousin's death. I watched him squirm pathetically as I noticed front of his trousers getting soaked. The fool pissed himself and he was begging for me to spare him. He even got on his hands and knees to kiss my boots which I re-warded with a solid kick to the face.

"You… you lied." He said as I leaned closer to him.

"And how is that?"

"Yo… yo… you do…" he stuttered, pissing me off more.

"Say it!!!" "You don't bleed… Do you?" This question caught me off guard. This pathetic piece of shit killed my cousin… and he asks such a stupid question. I was honestly baffled. Without saying anything, I stab my blade into his shin pinning it to the ground letting him scream in agony while I draw my dagger. I wipe a hand on his trousers so that he has a clear picture before dragging the blade across my left hand. Then I show him my dripping blood that mixed with that of black demon and holy light. He just stared in shock as I finally killed him, stabbing him through the skull.

"Steefas, your children can eat." I say before taking off into the sky. It didn't help, but its a start, I did two laps as I watched the village get engulfed under the sea of black. Hell hounds all converging in as they eat their fill before I turned, flying back to Katrina's palace. This village was no more…

As Janix flew off on the wind, he didn't notice the portal that had opened to the side of the building, nor did he notice the dark figure that was observing him for who knows how long…

CHAPTER 17

A Horrific Show

In hell during the slaughtering of the village

Confusion... vengeful... full of despair... these, were but a few of the emotions that souls were experiencing as they entered the realm of eternal punishment. The demons were getting flushed with the amount of extra souls that were entering all of a sudden as most were out making preparations for the coming wars. Today was supposed to be a slow day according to the ancient ledgers that Lucifer himself had witnessed the creation of.

The ledgers more commonly known as... the Book of Life, a text that was made popular by the old mortals of the golden age and decorated with pure gold etching and a seal of the old gods. This seal taking on the appearance of a hawk and an eye with a strip of silver cascading down the center as a ward against evil. Then there is the Book of Death. Created with the ideas that Anubis himself was to always watch over it. These texts though older in fashion, are the very foundations of humanities beginnings, ends, and in-betweens. Very few times have the ledgers ever been deviated from... times that usually meant that the lord him-self was punishing the mortals and wiping out entire civilizations from the face of his beloved creation, this was definitely one of those times.

When his father had created these books, it was with the purpose of leaving the lives that were supposed to be in heaven and hell separate... that is until he created the blow hard of a son—Jesus Christ— who gave the mortals a sense of ease that all sins are forgiven. Like the snap of ones fingers, that salvation is achievable without work... well, that may be a very thin partial truth. He did die on a cross, he was the ultimate lamb of his Father... but, what the Bible doesn't tell is that its not as simple as people make it out to be, for you see, Lucifer was the one who was now in charge of making sure that the damned souls all made it to the right location. This is done with the book of life, it was all the names of the souls that go to the Silver city... but not only that, it has all of the names that don't, all the names that join him and his demonic torturers down to eternal punishment. The ledgers give exact numbers of how many are supposed to die, where they die, and when they die.

This is why the death count was so unnerving, this was a massive and catastrophic event that left too many questions unanswered. "Cyjòk! Bring me the Orb of Odin!"

Cyjòk would have responded had it not been for the fact that when he agreed to serve the lord of all Evil itself, he had to forcefully remove his tongue. His eyes long since turned from that of a mortal to that of slits like a lizard with dripping fangs of poison. The rest of his appearance was in fact quite decrepit and misshapen. As he brought what his master demanded, he limped as his femur was long since broken. When he finally made it to the lord of Hell he un-covered the spherical orb that allowed him to see whatever it is he sought.

The orb was combination of glass, marble and runes. All of which tapped into ancient magic that held the answer too many questions that humanity was nowhere near ready for.

"BLAST IT YOU INFERNAL DEMON! You're dismissed."

Cyjòk gave a simple nod and slowly hobbled away as his master began the incantation of nordic origin to see into the realm of humans and the town in question.

To say Lucifer was in shock would be an under-statement, when the orbs misty haze cleared, it reviled to him what he asked, he saw hundreds of bodies littering the ground, the sound of dying men and women all around. Lucifer willed the orb to show him who was the cause of this and before him, severing the head of a young boy was non-other than Janix himself, tears streaming down his face and a fire burning in place of his eyes.

This was not the Janix he knew. This Janix held the look of a feral man. Of a man who has nothing left to live fore… Lucifer was about to teleport himself to the area be-cause it looked as if this was a one way mission that would result in his suicide… after everything that was accomplished and the alliances that have been forged, he could not let this happen.

However, just as Lucifer was ready, Janix finished off the last man who was screaming in agony leaving a haunting silence to reside over the land. Until Janix wings sprouted out of his back, the scene cut out suddenly as he heard Janix give Steefas and his children the ok to devour everything in the city.

Shock… this is all that Lucifer felt as he registered the creature that he had just witnessed… yes, not person, but a creature that the lord of hell didn't even recognize. This really didn't bode well with him as he sent a messenger to the upper world. Major events are playing out right now, but the simple question remained… What does this all lead to.

After finally getting over his initial shock, Lucifer left the pits of hell and journeyed to the upper realm. It was time for him to have a talk with RÿJunìc.

CHAPTER 18

A Daughters Requiem

THREE DAYS LATER

The last couple of days haven't been the best, once I returned to the fortress, I immediately informed Katrina of the situation and that I'll be off on my own for a while. Zoe, wherever the hell she was made the wise choice to stay away and leave me be. I could only catch glimpses of Ailani as I would walk around the corridors and Kailiana has shut herself away in her room. Turns out Egnachi had taken Axilious to a beautiful cliff face where we buried him. I was grateful for this as I didn't think I had the mental strength to do it myself. Bella's been keeping to herself other than when we switch off with babysitting Nae and I got a SITREP on Véchenti. Seems that Cain has taken up the role of teacher again and started training every able man and woman to fight.

But here in the fortress, I sat in my room playing with Nae who was now five years in bodily age. I was also attempting to teach her about the importance of meditation to which she refused to sit still long enough for. She was definitely Alex' daughter, preferring to be proactive in everything she did. Bella watched us as she ran around laughing as I attempted, failing miserably, too subdue her. Nae got up and started jumping on Bella's bed and I couldn't help but laugh. With a light smile on my face, I glanced at Bella who always seemed to have a look of sad-ness. It confused me to no end but when I would try to bring it up, she would always avoid the conversation, redirecting it to asking how I was doing which I also avoided. She also stopped calling me 'Nix' which was a shock at first but I never complained...

It took Andreas and Dehaas a full day and a half to fully recover from the battle with the Lizark, as RÿJunìc called it. Evidently, it was a creature of the old world when God was... experimenting with life, then he cast it into the realm of Ozîkai. Ozîkai is evidently an inter-dimensional hell that was created as an ultimate prison beneath hell which also just happens to be the prison of Cûrburōs. Upon hearing that, most of our spirits fell, as it just proved we had even less time than we thought we did.

It didn't matter though, as we were all emotionally drained from the past eight days of trial and loss. Not to mention that Kailiana has shut herself off from everyone. Releasing a sigh of aggravation, I got up giving Nae a hug and lightly ruffling her hair.

mmhhh' "Daddy!?!" She exclaimed to which I laughed. No matter how much I tried to get her to call me uncle, or even just Janix, she insisted on calling me that.

"Nae, just Janix is fine." I say chuckling. Knowing what she was about to say.

'mm mm', she rejected shaking her head. "Your daddy." She smiled at me brightly with a cute little expression. I looked over to Bella silently requesting help. Irritatingly though, she refused, smirking with mirth.

"Well, I have to go talk to auntie Katrina, listen to Bella alright." I said to which she nodded before asking Bella to pick her up.

"Why you do this to me Nix, I'll never know." I was halfway out the door she said this, but it was still enough to get me to pause in reaction.

"I said not to call me that..." I closed the door but couldn't help smirking as I left. Good damn that infernal knight. I walked through the corridors taking a few turns before I ended up outside Kailiana's room. What am I going to do with those two...

"Master?" Came the voice of Steefas startling the hell out of me.

"Steefas! What are you doing here?"

"I could ask you the same..."

"Just..." sighing, "She's been locked up for days man." I turn looking out the window that was part of the outer wall overlooking a vast Vally. "She may not like me much, but I swore to protect her as my own... shit... Steefas, she is my flesh and blood."

"No arguments from me master... its been one shit-ty situation after another, and... after what happened with your cousin..." he didn't finish, thing is... he didn't need to.

"I gave into my inner demons." I state before looking at him again. "Plain and simple, it's not marvelous, it's not heroic, fuck! It's not even justifiable." I state before looking back at the door. "But behind that door is a girl that's lost the only family she's ever known. I know what it's like man..." as I said this a rush of old memories flood my mind. "I know how it is to lose everyone... to not have anyone, and... if I can give that girl even a shred of comfort, then its my duty to try." I say before knocking on her door which opened instantly.

I found myself suddenly engulfed in a bear hug that threatened to crush me. She definitely has her father's strength. I think before she breaks the silence.

"Did you mean all that? Janix, did you actually swear to look after me... after all the crap I gave you?" She fired question after question at me before pulling way. "Well???"

"You were listening to us the whole time weren't you?" I ask before chuckling at her frown. "Of course I did, and Kailiana, I'm not even close to being the type of man that your uncle was, shit, I'm not even sure how the hell I'm supposed to be as a father. But I know that you're some-thing special, and I want to help you grow in any way I can... if you'll let me..." I state. It was the truth, Steefas stood off to the side just watching us with a wolfish grin. She walked over to the window herself, "I..." I heard her stutter before holding her arms close to her chest. "I never knew my mother..." she stated, "I'm sure as hell not ready or keen about accepting you as my father, Janix." She continued looking out as my face fell in to a frown of sorrow. Yet, upon noticing my frown she added, "I'm not opposed to having you as a potential friend though." I looked up to see her smirking and I just couldn't help feeling relieved when I heard that.

"I think I can accept that." I answer with a smirk before a deep chuckling from Steefas interrupted. "Say..." calling Steefas over. "Have I ever properly introduced you to him?" I asked throwing a thumb over my shoulder.

"Never had the pleasure."

"Well, please allow me to introduce Steefas, King of the Hellhounds, Lord of Shadow and Fire, also a real pain in my ass." I finish, earning a nip from him. "You know it's true." I laugh as Kailiana smirked.

"Pain in your ass eh, I think we'll get along just fine." My face paled as I recognized that look, it was the same look Ailani got whenever she got a mischievous plan to fuck with me.

"He's such a hansom wolf." She said before reaching out to pet him which he accepted gratefully.

"I like this one master, at least I didn't have to threaten her like your old mate." He said laughing but earning an odd look from Kailiana.

"Kailiana…" I tried but she cut me off, "Just Ana, if we're to get over this… situation be-tween us, might as well let you call me by my nick name that… uncle use to use." I nodded saddened at the memory of my dead cousin but I also noticed the tears that she tried to hide as well.

"Alright Ana, well… just know that you have someone to talk to, if you want."

"Yeah… thanks…" well, it was nice to know this was just as awkward for her as it was me. Oi, this was going to take a lot of time…

"Err… Steefas, we're needed with Katrina, I've put her off long enough." I stated, giving Ana a nod before leaving.

CHAPTER 19

War Council

An Unspoken Challenge

Walking away from Ana, Steefas and I proceeded to bicker. Not about anything of importance, just random miscellaneous topics. It continued like this until we ended up at the thrown room. However, instead of open, the huge doors were closed tonight. Yet they didn't obscure the massive cloning that was heard from with in. Not clanging like the clash of sword fighting, but a noise like that of many warriors in the room who are compressed together. I had seen and heard these sounds once before. It wasn't a good sign. It was the sign that there was over four hundred warriors crammed into this room. It was a sign that they were all adorned in armor and ready for battle. To make it worse, Steefas was growling, I felt the vibrations from deep within his throat as I reach over to pat him.

'Easy Steefas' I mentally spoke, not wanting to allow our voices to be carried to prying ears.

'Master, you and I both sense the power that's awaiting behind these doors.'

He was right of course, the amount of malicious energy was borderline overwhelming. It was the same consistency like that of Bella.

"Well, it's not like we have a choice." I tell him be-fore walking up to the doors and raising a hand to knock. As I was about to knock on the door, assuming that what-ever meeting was taking place with Katrina, we were al-ready late and something told me that Katrina would not be kind... even with what happened. It would probably not end with being interrupted welcomingly. Yet, before I could even touch them, the heavy Iron doors opened inwardly revealing three companies worth of Knights. All of them looking like a less glamorous version of RÿJunìc. There were rows upon rows of knights, all armed and armored, they were at attention and awaiting something... As for RÿJuníc, he was standing to Katrina' right, as she was seated in her thrown and appeared to be pulling all the stops as the was wearing her crown and the large diamond sword was next to her. To her left, was her dog hybrid that eyed everything with curiosity. In the corners of the thrown room, I noticed the six massive hell hounds that appeared to be the acting guardian angels. They were all of different colors, but they all shared one look of determination, they all had that look of pride that every hound I've meet held. They watched us enter the room, giving light bows of acknowledgement to Steefas.

As one, all of the warriors turned their gazes to-wards myself and Steefas.

'One hell of a party huh Master?'

'You can say that again.'

"Katrina?" I started only to get rudely interrupted by a young looking female hound.

"That's Lady Katrina you little welp!" The leftmost hound in the corner of the room snarled, earning herself a look of irritation from Steefas who simply growled a warning. I ignored the young hound of course, as she was obviously misguided in who she thought she was addressing.

With a confident look, I continued, "I was informed that you wished to speak with us, though I can see, we appear to

be in an even bigger meeting than I previously anticipated."
I was heavily analyzing the warriors who parted for me as I
approached the center of the thrown room.

"You are right Janix, as you will find out. RÿJunìc, you may
continue with the introductions."

"Aye Mi'lady."

"Knights of Hell!" RÿJunìc' voice echoed as it was projected
throughout the room. Once again, the knights snapped
to attention as their General spoke. "Here before you is the
legendary Lord Janix," this sent some of them into pure disarray,
"the very same Janix that fought with and defeated our second
finest knight in the Legion." This silenced the entire room, I
could even hear the whimpering of the hell hounds who now
that they understood who I was. "This meeting that we are
gathered for, is in accor-dance with the articles created by lord
Lucifer himself. This is contingency operation 666." Once again,
the room was sent into pure disarray as the knights broke all
formality and spoke their displeasure.

"How can this be?" A knight questioned.

"We lost nearly the entire legion last time we entered that
forsaken cavern." A thin looking knight ex-claimed from the
front.

"If this is really *the* Lord Janix, then there should be a
demonstration of power?" A stocky knight exclaimed from the
center of the formation.

"He doesn't look so tough, how are we supposed to follow
someone who looks as weak as this... this mortal does." That
last one seemed to get a reaction out of RÿJunic as he drew his
sword slamming it on his breastplate, silencing the whole room.
The knights all stepped away from the warrior who spoke out
of turn.

"YOU DARE QUESTION MY WORD ABOUT
LORD JANIX!!!" RÿJunìc' voice reverberated throughout
the hall as two knights pushed the warrior to his knees. "TO

QUESTION MY WORDS IS TO QUESTION THAT OF LORD LUCIFER HIMSELF!!!" He continued, stepping down from the place he was next to Katrina. I suddenly had a bad feeling as I prepared to act. Something was about to happen that I couldn't let continue. "THE PENALTY... IS DEATH!!!" My eyes widened in shock as he was about to strike down the supporter.

Pity, poor fool looked as if he had just accepted his fate, this was not going to happen. Steefas who understood what I was about to do, instructed the other hounds to stand down as my wings erupted from my back and I appeared with my blade stopping his. When our blades made contact, there was a small shock wave as both blade had a tinting aura of black and red. Both attempting to take control. As if they wanted us to fight until there was only one victor. The entire legion seemed to be torn, some wanting to draw weapons and others holding them back. If a fight was to take place here and now, then there was no doubt that there would be hell to pay from both sides. I knew that Steefas had the command of all six hounds as he appeared at my side growling menacingly at RÿJunìc. The six hounds formed a defensive circle around us as RÿJunìc and I stared each other down. Yet... there was no anger, no malicious intent in his eyes... it was simply, I don't even know what type of emotion he seemed to have.

"RÿJunìc! There is no need for such unpleasantries in my palace." Came the stern voice of Katrina who looked more bored than anything else. "The three of you, SHEATH YOUR WEAPONS!"

Obeying, we both did as she said and the legion stared at us in shock. "Do you see!" RÿJunìc exclaimed to the watching soldiers. "He not only blocked my attack, but he also commands the lord of hell hounds who turned our security against us, and what more. Bella herself has shown up to assist him if this had gotten out of hand." It was then that I noticed Bella was indeed behind him and appeared to be re-sheathing a dagger. When the hell she showed up, I didn't know, but it was reassuring that she appeared to be on our-side for the moment.

'Steefas, it's ok, just keep an eye on everything please, thanks for the back up.' He looked at me. Offering a brief nod in understanding, he then proceed to the corner of the leftmost hound who seemed to be squirming in her corner now. Upon sitting down, she flinched under his stern gaze.

"*Thanks.*" I mouthed to Bella who nodded back.

"Why can't we leave you anywhere Janix?" A very amused looking Andreas voiced from the shadows, with him was Lara and Valenzuela. Alright, now this is getting weird.

"Katrina? What the hell is this meeting about?"

"Isn't it obvious Janix?" Came the voice of Lucifer, who morphed from behind the thrown.

"This is an official War council." Dehaas stated landing next to me with Arkain.

"And like the last one, all hands are needed for what we're about to undertake." The Lycan King Hägrīs said stepping out of a portal.

"But you'd have known that if you were actually on time." The voice of Ailani cut in. She still looked pissed, but she at least wasn't attempting to kill me… for now. My heart did stop for a beat though, she looked absolutely stunning in her black armor tinted with white streaks. It seems that she has finally readopted her original fighting style. "Now Sister, no more out of you, we need to be civil in this meeting." Ailani looked like she wanted to argue, but a look from Katrina stopped anything she had to say and quite frankly, I was thankful. Now was not the time for our drama. I will need to introduce her to Kailiana and Nae though… I'll need to talk to Katrina about that. Not only that, but I need Alex here. As a father, and a husband. He deserves to be with his daughter… a hell of a lot more than I ever did…

CHAPTER 20

Plans and Introductions

HOURS LATER

After what seemed like an eternity, the long and arduous meeting was over. The leaders were all calling for an all out attack as they wanted to take care of this being right away. However, ideas of a frontal attack would be suicide for our forces. Even if there was a gamble worth taking, it would need be one good enough to risk my kids' lives for. Nae may be the daughter of Alex and Ailani, but she's just as much my daughter now, I will let Alex do his part as the legitimate father, however I will be the one to properly train her. Speaking of Alex, I walked over to Andreas with a plan simmering in my mind.

"Andreas!" I yelled out upon noticing he was about to vanish into the shadows again.

"Janix?" With a raised eyebrow, I came back out of the shadows as well as Lara and Val.

"Janix mi amigo." Lara came up engulfing me in a bone crushing hug. "Its been too long." Val came up to me and just gave me a fist bump. Simple but meaning full to us.

"What can we do for you Janix?" Andreas asked getting to the point quickly.

"It's Alex, I understand that he's a general in ours armies, but he needs to be here... with his family. Is there..." Andreas raised his hand for me to stop. I was about to question him when he nodded to Valenzuela who vanished into the shadows only to reappear three seconds later with a very confused and nauseous looking Alex.

"Janix, I consider you a brother, maybe not by blood, but you've proven that you're trust worthy and anything you need, my legions are at your disposal." Andreas said to me leaving me shocked.

"As are my Knights!" RÿJunìc chimed in walking towards us. I was absolutely speechless. No words seemed appropriate for the occasion and I couldn't do anything but give them both a smile. They both nodded to me in understanding before letting me take Alex to look around the area.

"We must take our leave Janix, I will be in touch as soon as we have more information." With that, the three of them disappeared into the shadows leaving me Alex and RÿJunìc alone.

"Janix... where the hell are we?" A very miffed Alex asked.
"You are..."

"WHY ARE YOU IN MY PALACE!!!!" A very angry Katrina asked causing Steefas and I too flinch. The color in Alex face seemed to drain as he realized who he was in the presence of.

"I... I..."

"I brought him here Katrina, he deserves to be with his *WIFE* and child. It's not right to keep that from him." At the mention of Ailani, Alex stood straighter and looked at me with hope. "Have you seen her? How is she, what's be-come of her?"

"And why would you bring him here without letting me know?"

"My apologies," I stated with a simple nod, "but he was brought here without me being given time too actually make you aware of what I wished to do." I reasoned while gesturing to the shadow that had the hint of val still dissipating.

Katrina looked us both over after before rolling her eyes and giving the ok for him to stick around.

"JACOB!!!" Katrina called her servant, "Get this man a room, I seriously doubt that my sister will want any contact with him at this moment."

"Ma'am" the servant stated with bow before grabbing Alex belongings that fell out of a shadow.

"Janix," Katrina sighed, "better catch the boy up with everything that's happened so far." I gave her a nod while taking notice that Alex had a weird look on his face. "Ailani! Come, we have much to discuss." Alex perked up and was about to try and run to his wife until I put up a hand signaling him to stay where he was.

"What more could we poss..." Ailani noticed Alex behind me and instantly turned away. I didn't blame her, we're the two men who kept her life in a lie. She's already tried to murder me, and she's never met either of her children who are already training for the next war that is... sure to end up being the death of us all.

"Come! Alex, we also have much to discuss." I rounded for the door dragging him with me. It was clear he didn't agree with what was happening, but he didn't fight me either, not that he could, but he understood that some-thing major was happening.

"After Ailani and I were tossed into the portal by Dehaas," I began while we were in the corridor of braziers. "We ended up in this forest on the other side of the iron mountains." The sun was going down and the torches now started to blaze more to illuminate our walkway. "We were ready to hike and make our way to the base until... she started questioning me."

"What... do you mean?" He looked at me with an unreadable expression.

"Before we were tossed, Dehaas said that it was time for us to tell her." I was sure that Alex was in shock right now. As it was I who told him that we can't let Ailani find out about what happened. Stopping in front of the door to my room "What was I to do Alex? She's needed for this final battle. I hate this as much as you do."

"I understand Janix." He said as dread filled his voice. "But... when you left...Lani, what happened to our child?" I grew a massive smirk. Opening the door and ges-turing for him to enter.

"Keep in mind that she's been aged approximately five years by the Roving Angels." I entered after him and... the sight which greeted us was, certainly an interesting one. Bella with a pink bow in her hair was hunched over by a little table 4 sizes too small for her as Nae was gifting her tea and using one of the many daggers to cut a crumpet in two.

"Will you pass the sugar Madame." She asks with a light laugh until she laid eyes on us.

"Aa.... aa... Janix!" She exclaimed as her face turned a deeper shade of crimson.

"Now, now! Please don't let us interrupt your important tea party! Alex don't you think your daughter has made an amazing hostess."

"Now Janix, what have you been teaching her!" He said in mock irritation. "Letting her host her own parties now! You know better." He bellowed in laughter.

"Do you think that they would allow us to join their private party?" I just couldn't help it. The situation was too damn amusing as Bella stood bidding us a good night and giving Nae a little pat on the head.

"Daddy! Who tis?" Nae asked with a head cocked. Alex for the fifth time tonight looked at me in shock as my face fell.

"Now, please understand that I've been trying to teach her. That I'm her uncle, nothing more. But she won't see reason. That's one of the primary reasons that I had them bring you here in the first place." A look of sadness filled his eyes as he gripped my shoulder. Tears welled in his eyes as he knelt to his daughters' height. Eyes Locked on her, never wavering. Nae kept looking between the two men as she had no idea what to think about the whole situation. Nor did she understand that before her was in fact, her biological father.

"D… did you name her?" He asked with a wavering voice.

"Dänai" Was my simple response as he engulfed her into a hug. She stood there arms limp as she was unsure how to react to the strange man, but she knew that he meant no harm. As Janix would have killed anyone attempting to get close enough to harm her.

"Dänai, I know this will be difficult to under-stand… but I'm your father." She simply held a look of indifference before blinking my direction. I nodded encouragingly, trying to convey the unspoken message.

"No!" Nae exclaimed shaking her head and pulling away from him, running to my side. I sighed before looking down at her with a sad expression. Putting a hand on her shoulder before kneeling to her height, I looked her in the eyes. About to explain who Alex was… even if it was to be painful for both her and I. Yet, before I could even begin.

"Janix." Came the stern voice of Alex. I looked up to him, noticing an odd look of resolve and defeat. "Janix, just…" He sighed.

"Its fine. Her hearts been touched by you." He took on a wistful look before forcing a very small smile. "Funny how you seem to have that effect on people… She looks to you as a father now, and… I owe you for everything…" in full honesty, it looked as if he was about to be sick, I under-stood though, even as he continued.

"…even being alive right now. Getting to be with Ailani… she meant so much to you." I understood what he was getting at, however it did nothing to nullify the shock I was experiencing as Alex spoke with wavering conviction. Saying it or not, he was gifting his daughter to me…

"Alex... I can't..."

"YOU CAN and you must!" He said before grabbing the collar of my cloak. "You're the strongest being we have here!" His eyes were wild like that of a man who's gone insane. "You're the only one I trust who would be able to protect my... who can protect Dänai!" I simply stared at him, processing his words. He was actually using logic... even in his wild state. It was nuts; yet, it was clear that he wasn't going to take no for an answer.

"*Damn it all Alex!*" I exclaimed quietly so not to freak out Nae. "Alright, I'll do it, but you will be in her life too." He looked slightly shocked at what I said but smiled. "Even if it's as her uncle."

"Deal, and thank you." I nodded before looking down at his hands.

"Mind getting your hands off me?" I said it with only a hint of edge in my voice. I was honestly amused, but also, the last time he grabbed me like this I put him in a head lock and instincts could only be suppressed for so long.

He actually looked miffed by my statement until he realized what he was doing and the color once again drained from his face. "Janix... I'm sorry..." he tried before I raised my hand silencing him.

"You're a man who wants his daughter taken care of, that said, you need to reintroduce yourself." I left no room for debate, even though he had already agreed two my terms. He gave me a simple nod before doing as I said.

Just like that, young little Nae had a new uncle.

CHAPTER 21

Dark Realizations

It was a few days after Alex and Nae had accepted each other. It was slow but they were building a bond with one another. I couldn't help but smile, as Alex got to experience the few years that Nae had as a child. Ailani was still a avoiding both of us as it was and I wasn't even sure if she knew of the existence of Nae or Kailiani. I was sitting in a corner of the room watching the Alex and Nae interact while I mulled over how to approach Ailani. That was all but thwarted when Steefas showed up at the door allowing me to discreetly remove myself from the room.

"What is it Steefas?"

"Master, Lucifer and RÿJunìc wish to have a word with you as well as Rústĭcar."

Sighing, I was pretty sure I knew what this was about. I'm sure that the souls I sent to hell would have raised some suspicion.

"Very well, lead the way oh MIGHTY Lord of hounds." I said before smirking at Steefas discomfort as he hated when I used his actual titles. With a low growl "Imma bite you for that later master." His eyes flashed red as he humorously bared his teeth at me.

"I'm sure you will man, but until then what chamber would Lucy and Rústĭcar be staying in right now?"

"Last door on the left, just past the chamber of Rústīcar. Very well, I'll see you later... Maybe." I said with a chuckle at the end.

Walking to the door way I couldn't help but not feel this trickle of worry, after getting subdued so easily by Lucifer, I noted just how weak I really am. And that didn't change even with how far I've come. Just... seeing the last of my family get murdered in such a way made me lose control. I saw nothing but red.

"Janix!!!" Exclaimed RÿJunìc I simply gave him a polite nod.

"Its been a few days RÿJunìc. How are the knights?"

"Please, you and I both know you aren't here to talk about my administrative duties with the Knights of Hell. I need to hear about this massacre that you never invited me on!!! I mean, not just anyone can do that to an entire village of scoundrels. Plus the women and children too!!! Damn! That's awesome my man." RÿJunìc praised as the pit in my stomach seemed get deeper and deeper than it already was. But as RÿJunìc was rambling, I was focused on Lucifer the whole time. As RÿJunìc talked, I was trying to gage Lucifers reaction which was staying entirely stoic during. It was very unnerving to see his expression... well, lack thereof. I didn't know what to say in full honesty.

—I mean, even you who are reading this, what do you say to the being whose possibly more powerful than you and staring into your very soul—

"RÿJunìc, that's enough. I must ask you to leave us now while Janix and I... discuss the issue at hand." Lucifer quietly explained. RÿJunìc just had a quick look of irritation before he bowed to his lord, walking away. As he disappeared into a shadow Lucifer began to draw a series of hieroglyphs in the air which slowly expanded and began glowing gold before forming like a repetitive streak al around the room. It was not unlike that of the runes in the chamber of Rústīcar. As he finished the last symbol, Lucifer fixed his dress shirt before look at me finally.

"There, now we won't be interrupted. Also, I'm sure that you're curious to what form of spell casting that was." At my nod he simply sighed before explaining. *"They are the runes of an ancient culture that was predominant even before our father began his crusades."* To say I was shocked would be an understatement. I couldn't help but wonder what else was still out there. Rústīcar... Cûrburõs...

"I..." Lucifer never gave me the chance to respond as he continued.

"It is unclear to all but father what happened to that civilization. But their ways can still be found to this day by scholars, and miners." He paused for a moment to allow me to fully process the scale of what he was saying. This was beyond what I had though was going on. But... why the secrecy???

"You know you're lucky." He said breaking me out of my thoughts. *"That village wasn't meant to be destroyed for another year."* Sighing he trailed off walking over to a lit brazier and grabbing a coal that was still lit. *"Most of the souls have gone to where they belong. But I'm still sifting though the names and placing the idiots in their rightful place of punishment."* He paused staring at me. *"You can breathe now!"* With that I released a breath that I hadn't realized I as holding.

"But... I killed..." With the snap of his fingers, Lucifer conjured up two chairs. Effectively cutting me off before he continued.

"Have a seat! Consider it doing me favor. Saves me the trouble of having to plan a raid, a disaster or anything else weird." Lucifer replied cutting me off. *"Now, with that said Janix. As I stated before, you were very lucky that you didn't alter fate or the plans of father. Trust me, been there and done that. I only got tossed out of heaven and thrown into Hell as its ruler. YOU! On the other hand will get a far greater punishment."* He ended with a hand on my shoulder while glancing at the ceiling as if waiting for God to make himself known or to do something divine.

"Lucifer… I," He once again silenced me with the face of his hand and continued, *"but that is water under the bridge no harm done, thank you for saving me the paper work of manifesting a massacre, now, let's talk about your training."*

Janix just looked at him like he was insane, just what could the lord of Hell be planning.

"Oh! One more thing though."

Lucifer then pulled out a dagger that seemed to give off a brilliant glow. Like that of the moon on a cloudless night.

This, is the dagger 'Stærkah'. It was forged in the pits of hell by a sorceress who murdered Lycans and Djinn. Then merged the bloods together into this blade, hand crafted from a stone that fell from the moon." As he wielded it, Janix observed the trail of light that it left. Like that of a shooting star in which one would look upon and make a wish.. However, one thing was left now, "Lucifer, although it is an interesting story, why are you telling me any of this? Why are your you showing me any of this?" It truly was magnificent, but who would wield such an unruly blade.

"Well, I am going to gift it to Kailiana. She is more than worthy of wielding it and my champion will not be under armed."

"Wait a minute… your Champion?" I asked. This was all just too much to take in suddenly. Who the hell said that Lucifer could claim my daughter as his Champion.

"But of course, seeing as things seem to be advancing the way they are. Seems fitting I claim her."

"And what the hell makes you think that I want her to be your champion? Or that she would even want to be your Champion?"

"Janix, I am the lord of Sin and Evil, King of Hell itself. Who wouldn't want to be under my servitude."

"Lucifer, I will talk to my daughter, and you will accept whatever answer she gives you, if you don't, then you will taste my Blade!"

"*Oh soooo dramatic. Fine, if that's how you wish to play it, but be warned, one of your daughters will be my Champion!*"

"We'll see about that you insufferable leach!" I exclaimed with hate... we eyed each other, the tension thick as could be. Then in an instant, we both just broke out into a fit of laughter between us. Lucifer explained that he did have intentions of running it by me and Ailani beforehand. As infuriating as the lord of hell is, he isn't such a bad being. Even if he's a little overly cryptic about his way of doing things...

CHAPTER 22

Teachings of Miracles

After the exchange of banter, we supernatural beings concluded the meeting with Lucifer opening a portal to Lord knows where before stepping through. Upon exiting, we ended up on the cliff side of a massive waterfall that seemed to be red as blood.

"Don't look so worried Janix, it's only red water." Lucifer soothed my thoughts as I was peering very worriedly at it. *"Your training, is going to be utilizing it actually."* He said as he raised his right Angelic hand before sending a bolt of light into the center stopping the water in its flow and stopping the waterfall. *"As you know, we Angelic beings have the ability to create miracles."* With that he raised his left hand allowing a surge of demonic energy to shoot at an area of land behind us. Upon shooting it, there was a loud crash as bolts of black energy shot in the land and created an entirely new river that led off to nowhere.

"This is the utilization of both Angelic divine power and dark magic. Commonly confused with the magic of demons but in reality could be trained by mages of this world to be utilized. Your former girlfriend almost mastered the power of divine magic but now she's out of balance with her power as its not had an outlet for the last few years." Lucifer explained.

"This is why when you witnessed her using her power against the golems, she lashed out with pure energy and a botched combination of dark magic mixing with di-vine power." To me, it all made an

odd amount of sense. That also explained the amount of weird powers that I seem to keep discovering while having no idea how I accessed them.

This Janix, is your training. Except you will do more than just created a river, I expect you to created an environment with your powers. Try not to take too long, we really don't have much time for it to go by longer." He then left in a portal and allowed the waterfalls to proceed falling as they normally did. I, on the other hand was simply baffled at the prospect of conjuring such divine power for personal use and the fact that Lucifer expected him to create an entire environment was impossible… yet, I couldn't help but wonder. Taking a seat on the rock face in a meditative state, I allowed my senses to branch out and feel all of the natural energies around me, the energies of the universe. I felt the rumble of the land from the mighty force of the waterfall as water flowed down. I could sense the electric energy that surrounded all beings in the world, the freshness of the air allowed me to see into my subconscious, the inner light that was divine Angelic powers. After a time of sitting, I allowed my right hand to rise and felt a tingling sensation that seemed to wrap around my lower arm all the way the base of my elbow. I knew this to be the divine energies that I was now manipulating and just waiting to be expunged from my being. With an index and middle finger, I pointed towards the constant flow of the rapid waterfalls, before thrusting out my arm and shooting a solid beam of energy. Thus creating a wall of light that once again stopped the water from falling. However, just as quickly as I created it, a bead of sweat fell from my brow as I felt the intensity. Intensity of the force that the water was pushing and trying to break through. It was then that I lost my focus and the water came crashing down again.

Damn I thought falling to my knees, panting in exhaustion. The amount of force that's required to hold it, as well as the stamina combined with how much energy I'm using is outrageous. How the hell am I supposed to be able to manifest all of this energy and create a new environment... Catching my breath, I rose from my knees before getting into a stance again. With two legs slightly bent, my right hand raised again as I channeled al of the energies. Yellowish light surrounded my right forearm and a solid line began to wrap around it like a snake until it ended just under that of my elbow. I was able to channel it once again into that of a solid beam except this time I forced more energy to maintain it as I looked non at the florescent yellowish white beam that stopped the water, this time it didn't feel that bad however, as I allowed some of my demon energy to fly and fuel the light wall that suddenly held a purple tint to it. Readjusting my stance, I angled my body so that my right arm was maintaining the wall of light with my legs bent and feet solidly placed on the ground, I raised my left arm. I felt the atmosphere change as the smell and taste of ozone suddenly filled the air, flashes of dark electricity began to spark out of my left hand, however, just as I was about to cast it with my fingers all focused on the landscape that Lucifer had used, there was a blast and it felt like my entire arm was ripped apart. The next sensation that I felt was that of free falling. The entire left side of my body felt as if it were on fire while the right side felt cold as ice and completely damp. I felt blind as I couldn't see anything around me, there was nothing but darkness, darkness and the pain. Then, everything ceased and I was enveloped in unconsciousness.

DREAM STATE

For a moment I wasn't able to comprehend just where the he'll I was as I started to drift through he expanse of darkness and nothingness, that is until I felt my feet touch the ground. It was as if there was a light silhouette around me yet it only illuminated two meters around me in every direction, the land that I was on was solid rock, that is until I took a few steps in a random direction and slipped into a deep... pond? Water hole? I didn't know, all I knew was that I was suddenly head deep in blood and this time I knew for sure that I was in blood. My body spasmed in sheer panic as I reached for the land that I slipped away from only to find that the water was now moving, this hole was suddenly an ocean and I was stranded in the middle of it. It began to rain, and the waves got higher. There was nothing I could do as lightning flashed illuminating the ocean and the mighty form of Cûrburōs standing over me.

His monstrous appearance walking through the waves that barely touched his waist. This time however, he didn't talk to me, he just kept walking until he passed me and kept moving. The sky was once again illuminated to reveal that the bolts of energy weren't lightning, but in fact Lucifer and Andreas battling the massive beast. They were sending massive amounts of power and all it did was earn them growls from the immortal of destruction and death. I noticed that it still had both of its chains on but they seemed a deeper shad of rot. Now, I don't know much about the powers of ancient magic, more am I even going to try and comprehend the amount of power that was required to create them. But they definitely didn't look the right color that they are supposed to be. It was then I saw the left most head with its chain almost completely worn through, it was clear. The magic was fading and rapidly at that. As I watched the battle rage, Cûrburōs brought up a mighty arm to swipe at Lucifer who was charging up energy to combat him only for Andreas to fly and knock him out of the way. In doing so, Andreas took the brunt of the impact and I could only watch as Andreas was cut down from the sky, I watched as he fell into the blood waters and then... darkness enveloped me again.

I awoke with a shock and my eye clamped shut again complete pain. It felt as if my entire left side was on fire, my body paralyzed and in an odd state of burning and freezing.

Opening my eyes finally, I took in my surroundings, I was washed up on some bank and there appeared to be a waterfall behind me. I tried to move, getting up on my good but still aching right arm only to slip and fall in to the damn rocks once again sending sheer pain into my body as I cried out in agony. Just great, first I was left to attempt a new task that I knew nothing about, and now I'm here in pain and judging by the fact that I'm not healed yet, I sustained a great magnitude of damage to myself physically and spiritually.

"Gods fucking damn it!!!" I screamed in pain and anger into the heavens. I was paralyzed… I was in pain, I couldn't move without being in excruciating pain that even I can't withstand. So what is it that I need to do… is it possible that I witnessed the death of Andreas?

What was I supposed to make of such a dream??? Can I believe that he's gone? There's no possible way, he's the son of the Morning Star…Yet, in the back of my mind, I couldn't help but realize that everything that I had witnessed from the astro plain was in fact real. But that just added to the mystery of various things that were happening in the current age. On top of this, there is so much that I need to learn still.

These were the thoughts that flowed while I was in the process of healing and regaining my angelic power. I couldn't feel my body anymore as I was still partially in the water. The cool water soothing my burned and scaring skin. Yes… this time I would be permanently scared, as even I can tell that the damage is extensive. Still numb with pain, I began falling back into the comfortable abyss of darkness. Yet, even as the world blacked out, I suddenly felt weightless, weightless and there was noise. As if some unknown being were carrying me, moving me, soothing me as. This is all that I felt, as darkness fully overtook me in a calming sleep.

CHAPTER 23

Total Displacement

Time is but displacement... displacement within the natural universe in which we live. I've seen exactly what it is that God himself created. Two years ago when Jehovah graced my grandfather with his presence explaining the purpose of this. What is it that must be done though...

PAIN

My numerous thoughts were broken and interrupted by immense pain in my left side as it seemed that fire was re-igniting itself and though I couldn't move, I felt some-thing... no, someone manipulating my right leg and messing with my wrist. I wanted to yell out, to scream at them to stop fucking touching me. Yet the only thing I could even muster was a... light whimper. This seemed to be enough though, even if just for a moment it seemed that whoever it was let go of me and moved back. That is until I felt a soft hand graze my right cheek, and tender lips touch my fore-head.

Wha... what is this person doing? In the blackness that was my consciousness, I couldn't fully comprehend what is going on. Only that it seemed that this mystery person held some form of affection towards me... at least enough that they hope I'll be okay. This was as much as I was able to analyze before fully going unconscious.

Dream Realm

That's when I saw it, the strange tunnel in front of me, a rotating spiral of energy and galaxies. FUCK!

"You've made quite the mess of things my boy." Came the voice of one being I didn't think I'd hear from again. Come to think about it, I think I'd prefer it if I didn't hear that voice again… with a sigh, I finally responded to the Creator.

"And you've all but abandoned your creation," I said into the open space of nebulas and galaxies before looking at him. "Why do you make yourself known now???"

"All in good time Janix, but for now, it's time you continue your training. You and a few others will be displaced in a pocket realm where time is relative. Now. AWAKE!!!" Just like that, I felt the ever so familiar feeling of falling through air as light at the bottom of my cavern got closer.

"ARHHHHHH!" I yelled out bolting up grasping a dagger and taking in my surroundings. It was strange because I wasn't sure where the dagger came from and yet, it was as if it were naturally here. I enjoyed the idea that I could conjure up a weapon at random, yet the person under me, the one who was now looking at me in fear, none other than Bella who held such a strange expression. One that I couldn't fathom to read… one that I didn't want to read. It was faint, almost smothered by the fear and surprise, but it was there nonetheless. I use to see it in Zoe's eyes, and Ailani's eyes before, before they turned their backs on me. Never again, I removed the blades pressure from her throat as the adrenalin that coursed through me receded.

Like a piercing arrow, pain shot through my left arm and leg as I crumpled to the ground in a low whimpering pain. Bella, who had regained her composure, although there was still a light blush on her face, got back to her feet before taking in a breath and smirking at me.

"Dumb ass!" She said picking up some of the medicinal herbs that was knocked down when I assaulted her. "Here I was trying to be nice." The former Knight of Hell commented.

"After the amount of Hell I've experienced!" I said in pain.

"Hell?" Bella asked with a light cackle. "Until you've been part of the group that's had to monitor him every year... You know nothing of real hell!" When she said that, I didn't need anymore explanation to whom or what she was talking about. In fact it was her mentioning that monstrosity that brought back the dreadful memories of the dream I had. A dream I just knew to be reality, still though. As I watched her pick up the items carefree and relaxed, I couldn't help but feel the dread. It's quite possible that we just lost a very powerful ally... no, not possible, even as I thought about it. I knew it was a fact, I really did see him fall, and now, I need Bella's opinion.

"M.... Bella" I grunted out, it was a lot more painful than I thought it would be. "Andreas! Fell, in dream."

"Shhh. Tell me later, though I'm fairly sure I already know what it is that you're trying to tell me." She told me with a solemn expression. "You must rest and prepare for your trials ahead Nix, there is very little time, as we speak, Dehaas and Arkain are aging young Nae." My eyes widened at this, as she wasn't supposed to get aged again for another week. I wanted to question her more about what's been happening, but then I felt my eyelids get heavier until I was enveloped in darkness again. Yet not before I felt the familiar sensation of lips being pressed on my forehead.

"Trust in yourself young Janix! Things are not as they appear." The supernatural and ethereal voice said as images of the galaxy swirled around a familiar cave that I appeared to be in. ***"Times are changing, and though you denied it, you must accept you're calling as the new Lord!"*** The cavern shuddered and suddenly I was expunged into the light before I fell through. However,

instead of waking up like I've been doing, I was once again in the presence of the Cûrburõs.

"Speaking with the Creator now are we?" His raspy voice sounded in my mind, at this point I just sat there, his very essence was over baring and I could do nothing, so why bother.

"Well it matters not whether he speaks or not." One of the heads commented.

"It seems that he's accepting his fate, as he should," The three heads continued to speak to themselves.

"Yes, he is realizing the he stands no chance against us. Especially when we devoured that petty Roving Angel."

The dream began to shudder as the great beast let loose a horrific laugh causing the environment to literally shatter around me. Effectively waking me up panicked and sweating.

I couldn't see anything out of my right eye this time... slowly, with my good left hand, I raised it until I felt a face wrap around the right side of my face. Glancing down, I noticed the entire right side of my body was wrapped in bandages. Directly across from me, I noticed that Bella was sound asleep with an older looking Nae, both of which were snuggled into Steefas fur while Kailiana stood watch with a burned out fire by her feet. Seems everyone came out to join me this time. Sitting up, there was still a dull and throbbing pain in my right side but it was doable.

Slowly, I stood before limping over to Ana who appeared to be deep in thought.

"Anything of interest?" I asked breaking Ana from her deep thinking.

"Father? You're awake!" She said before looking me up and down before smirking. "You look like *crap*." To which I rolled my eyes.

"Remind me to teach you how to manipulate the spiritual energies of both angelic and demonic, then we'll see how you feel afterwards." I jested with a light chuckle, although I was still in pain. It was good to express humor again.

"Yeah, I think I'm good dear father, after all, I was primarily raised by the angels so I doubt that I have that kind of power anyways." Scoffing, I just rolled my eyes.

"Please, you're the daughter of a **Halfbreed** and the most powerful Sorcerous the world has known since the creation of mankind. If anything, my daughter would be twice as strong as I am." I said laughing before I realized what I'd said. "I mean…" looking down at here, I couldn't help but notice how she'd gone rigid. Really I had no idea how to save myself. After all she'd been the one to tell me that she wasn't sure about me, and that we still had a lot of growing to do. Yet, too my shock she just started laughing.

"I suppose my genetics are an interesting combination now that you mention it." She said before shooting a burst of light energy out of her right hand creating a small firework. I scoffed, "Interesting is putting it lightly, you're one of a kind Ana." As we finished our little banter, I couldn't help but grin at the fact we were bonding and growing on each other.

Looking back over at trio who looked so comfortable, the low rumble of Steefas breathing putting a sense of calm around us. My expression turned serious again.

"Tell me what I missed." I said to her as I remembered what the lord said to me previously.

"Honestly… we were all hopping that you could tell us. After a few Hours of you departing I, along with Bella and Nae there appeared here on the edge of this pond." She said before tossing another piece of wood into the crackling fire. "We found you in quite a pitiful state, whatever type of training you were conducting damn near obliterated your essence. Dehaas was mad as hell. We treated your wounds of course, but then Bella told me about how you damn near took her head off." She explained with light chuckles here and there to which I smiled bemused at that before grimacing, knowing how she will find a way to make me pay for that. "Steefas showed up not long after we'd gotten situated." She smiled looking over at the massive wolf. "He was livid. Absolutely pissed about the fact that you had gotten so injured without him or any of his children around." I couldn't help but scoff at that, damn over protective Hellhound. It was after this that her expression got dark again.

"Father... I need to know, what happened between you too? She's been nothing but kind to me, helped raise me... sort of with Andreas and Dehaas. Hell, even my little sister adores her!" She said looking at me with pleading eyes to which I couldn't help but sigh. She was rightfully confused, our relationship... was a rocky one that didn't begin on the best of terms...

"Yet, you treat her like she's the bane of your existence, like..." I don't know what it was, but I snapped at this point.

"Like she wronged me in a way that I could never forgive?" She reeled at the amount of venom that came from me when I spoke. "Like I've seen her do atrocities that have ended entire civilizations? Or maybe the fact she's the murderer of my first love... Zoe!?!!!" I knew I'd gone too far and that my demonic aura was engulfing me in darkness. I knew my eyes were probably black and with gold halo's in the center. I sensed that Steefas was wide awake but forcing himself to remain planted in his spot as he moved his tail over Nae to shield her from anything un-becoming that Ana and Bella could handle.

"You haven't lived long enough Kailiana! You haven't seen the atrocities that can and have been commit-ted." With raw power I began to levitate as a crater began to form beneath me.

"Then tell me!" She yelled over with wind that was picking up. Whipping her hair all over. "I want to know!" By this time, Bella had also awoken and standing by Kailiana's side with a hand on her angelic sword. Steefas remained curled around Nae creating a shadow shield keeping noise and the elements that were whipping about from disturbing her.

My mind was damn near in oblivion, I had very little control as I began witnessing flashbacks of things long gone. The death of my Zoe, the taking of Ailani, the death of Ezekiel, the murder of my cousin, and at the center of all the other atrocities that I was witnessing from times long since passed. Was Myself... engulfed in hellfire, my pupils were black as night and my sword was drawn. I was surrounded by the villagers I massacred... not only them... but I was surrounded by my friends and old family... all looking at me with disgust.

"WHAT IS THIS!?!!" I yelled out as I observed the scene in front of me.

"I've told you before Janix... that time is but displacement, behold... what you could have been, and those that you would have killed if you chose the path of damnation..." The Creator explained, then in an instant, the scene rippled and in front of me was the same scene... but this time my body was impaled, Nae and Kailiana were crying around me as hell fire was slowly engulfing everything around them.

"Now witness, a possible future." God stated as I watched Cûrburõs spread hell and despair over the landscape. It was then that I noticed how Cûrburõs was walking toward Nae and Kailiana. I wanted to scream, to yell out for them to run and save themselves, but just as it seemed like one of the heads was about to clamp its jaws around my two daughters, the scene rippled and changed again. **"Remember what I told you, Time is relative... when you embrace total displacement."**

CHAPTER 24

Acceptance

The world around me was in chaos as anger blinded me. The lords comments made little sense as I tried to force myself to regain control. Kailiana and Bella both stood before me with Steefas protecting Nae.

Red... Red is all that I saw as black lightning struck around me, but not only this, there was heavenly light swirling around in a rotating vortex and I knew an angelic halo was above my head. I could feel the power intensifying as the speed of the heavenly and demonic energy combined into a low hum, halos in my eyes glowing brighter and I noticed a flash as Dehaas arrived to stop Bella from interfering. It appeared that words were exchanged as they all seemed to stare and watch me. The last thing I heard was a loud crack and then... nothing.

There was nothing but darkness for what seemed like an eternity. All the while I heard the soft calls of Kailiana, only they seemed so... distant away. That is until I saw a small light, no bigger than that of a sliver just making it through a crack in a wall. It was so beautiful, so peaceful. I wanted to reach out and touch it. But as I had these thoughts, I realized that it wasn't time. Turning around, there they were, my family, Ailani, Kailiana, Nae... all of my friends and allies. Ailani just looked at me with irritation before saying, "Really Nix, you let a little spat like we had dictate what happened to us?" Reaching her hand out, "I thought our love was stronger than that."

I tried to reach out and take her hand but it disappeared in to a black mist. Confused, I looked out at everyone else as Kailiana burst out laughing.

"DAD!!! The Hell was that???" She rolled her eyes at me before tossing me the blade I'd summoned before passing out... or whatever this is. As soon as my fingers grasped the hilt of the blade, she also vanished into black mist. Steefas was more forth coming with me as he walked up to me.

"Master, you need to let go of the past. You of all immortal beings should have realized that. I don't serve weaklings." He vanished into mist like the others before him. Leaving me more confused than ever. None of my other friends came up to me like the first three so I assumed that this was now my test... whatever the hell it was.

Silence, that's all that was around. Even as the village of Véchenti stood before me. I finally looked at the blade that Kailiana had tossed me. Realizing with a start, that it was engraved with one name. The name that brought me so much distain and hate. The name of Bella. Still this confused me... what the hell did it mean?

That is until I thought about what Ailani, Kailiana, and Steefas had said to me. That's when it clicked, how I realized the history they were really talking about wasn't just about not wanting to be hurt. But the unaccepting nature I'd adopted after being betrayed so many times. Al-though she probably didn't deserve it, the Lord saw fit to redeem her.

With a heavy sigh, I finally looked up to see Nae had walked up to me while I was in my thoughts. I thought she was going to say something, that is until she just hugged me. Taken aback, I just looked on as I felt the strange warmth of another. The sensation was almost for-eign to me, I hadn't felt it in a while. Even just standing here, I could feel my distain, hate and anger slowly fading... then everyone including Nae vanished into mist be-fore I was engulfed in darkness for a final time. That is until a light fell and landed right in-front of me. In gleaming white armor, she stood proud and with fury in her eyes. Not a cold fury of hate, but that kind of fury when you're in a competition with someone.

Bella shot me a smirk before extending her hand to me. I stared at her. All the pent up emotions finally expunged and gone. Leaving me with hollowness and... sadness. That is until I reflected on all that had just transpired. Then I saw the smiling faces of my long lost friends. All of them giving me a simple nod.

I reached out and took her hand. All of time seemed to stop as she continued to smirk at me. "Well it bloody took you long enough. Now wake up, we need to train."

With that simple statement, I shoot up once again, but this time drenched in sweat and I noted that my bandages have been changed and I was... shirtless... again.

"Finally back with the world of the living dad?" Came the distinct voice of my pride, Kailiana.

I looked myself over again when she said that, taking note that I was healing, it was a painful and slow process that would take time. "From there we've been camping out, although the sun rises and falls, I've noticed that the stars remain in the same place overnight, that was three days ago when I noticed them. Bella...well, actually in the morning she should explain it to you, we... found something while you went back under. According to her, we are in a time loop that will not let us advance farther than a mile away from the area."

In all honesty, this all fit with what the Lord had told me while I was out the first time. There was just one more thing that didn't make any sense to me.

Why were all three of them here???

I was about to question Ana about that very thing when suddenly I felt this pull of drowsiness almost over-take me once more and when I almost fell over...

"Whoa there father... I think you need to rest more. I shouldn't have pushed so hard with that question earlier... I promise I'll wake you at first light. I know how you are about that." Kailiana stated as she helped me lay down where I was previously. "You know father, tomorrow is my birthday." She whispered to me. I don't know if she thought I heard her or not but I definitely did and had to think of something. However all I could give her at this moment was a final nod before allowing dreamless slumber to overtake me.

CHAPTER 25

Peace and History

The next morning, I was woken up by a very energetic Nae who was literally jumping up and down crawling all over me trying to get me to stir. I pretended to stay asleep before jumping up myself and catching a very startled Nae in my arms before we both let out some boisterous laughter.

"Well Good morning little one, and just what are you doin crawling all over me this morning?" It was good natured but I was still curious although the sly look on Ana's face explained a good number of what I was asked. Especially when Nae glanced at her then down with a flushed look.

Walking over to them, I lightly tapped Bella whose hand reflexively shot to my throat in an attempt to choke me but my body was hardened and the simple act wouldn't affect me. Still, I couldn't help but smirk at a very confused Bella.

"Well good morning, sleep well?" I asked.

"Janix?!??" She asked back.

"Haha, yeah, I'm relatively feeling better now, though, think you could release me?" I asked holding the same amusement. She looked at me still perplexed until she lowered her gaze to my throat which was still being wrapped around by her strong hand. Eyes widening, her hand shot away from me as she held it close and she was now looking down embarrassed.

"Janix, I'm sorry…" she wasn't able to continue her apology as I let loose a loud, thunderous, and good natured laugh that seemed to resonate in the small valley we appeared to be in.

"I guess you could say that we're even now eh?" I reply with more laughter. She turned red before lightly smiling and joining in my mirth at the ridiculous situation we found ourselves in and even little Nae joined in our laughter.

"How has everyone been? I know I haven't been gone that long but it still feels like damn near eternity. We'll discuss the episode when I first woke up in a bit ok?" I asked setting a confused Nae down besides us. The others just nodded and Steefas hit me upside the head with his tail before letting a wolfish chuckle out which I returned in kind.

"It may not have been that long for you, but to us it's been three weeks in the modern world." Replied Bella. My head immediately shot to Ana who was looking down sheepishly.

"That's what I wanted to wait to tell you last night. We were getting so worried. And… well, Hell has been cut off for the last seven days in the real world." Kailiana in-formed me. That was news to me. Meaning that my first dream… damn…

"No… This can't be…" I looked down crestfallen. Looking back up at all three of them who each now held solemn expressions. Nae walked up to me before grabbing my hand.

"Andreas?" I asked.

"The news was brought to us just before we were brought here." Kailiana replied before looking down and I noticed a lone tear fall before she could hide it. "Father I'm sorry…" she began before I moved and engulfed her in a hug. "He and Dehaas… they weren't perfect, but they were all that I had growing up with uncle Axilious." It was cruel, but I now understood why she suddenly acknowledged me as her father. Her current father figures have dwindled to only Dehaas now… it also explained why her entire demeanor seemed to change… they bred her to be an assassin… they taught her how to be independent…

but what Andreas and Dehaas failed to teach her was that in this line of work, we will lose people. We will lose friends… family… in some cases everything we've ever known. She may have been raised and prepped to kill, but she was never taught how to let go, and this… Was an entirely new experience for her, one that she would never forget for the rest of her life. It comes down to what she does now though. So this is what they meant when I was told that I will have to teach both Nae and Kailiana.

Looking to the sky I released a sigh before asking the Lord for the wisdom to accomplish the tasks that I must now. The left side of my chest now damp with Kailiana's tears as she sobbed and released all the emotions that she attempted to suppress since she was able to cognitively think. Bella helped by grabbing Nae and holding on to her for me as I was able to now properly hug Kailiana who was finally understanding just how human she actually is.

"Why does it hurt so much?" She asked before looking up at me. Allowing my wings to extend, I sent a quick mental message to Steefas who was awake but wisely staying silent before taking off with my daughter in my arms. It was now that she learned.

"Ana, it's time for me to show you something." I said a quick spell combined with a prayer before we were teleported to a place I didn't want to remember. The village of Reypiere… the remains of it anyway.

"Father… what is this place?" A now very confused Kailiana asked. I refused to answer, as memories began to flood my mind. I was in a trance, as I flew us to a place I didn't want to visit again. The final resting places of my brothers in Arms.

"Kailiana," I began. "What were you told of the Reckoning?"

"Nothing, aside from you fought in it and were a hero to many" I couldn't help but sigh before letting out a light chuckle.

"That the hogwash that the Chickens with Angel wings told you?" She just nodded, not reacting to my little quip that I had for the Angels. "Well, I wasn't known as a hero… hell, if anything I was known for being the reason that my brothers were killed." Kailiana looked shocked but waited for me to continue. "Follow me."

We walked through the ruins of a few houses and then under a massive archway that held the faces of ancient warriors that originally conquered these lands. I created a ball of light as we passed into the darkness of the tomb. Images of the war flashed through my mind. The faces of my brothers as they each fell in battle. The battles that the villages didn't know about. That everyone believes I abandoned them... but its nothing compared to what really happened. The hell that was inevitable, the death that was to come.

We entered a cavern that was large enough to house an entire civilization—at one point it did— and all around us were the remnants of the defeated demon army which was bought down by my brothers. For me, was a painful reminder that I failed to do what I had sworn to before. Thus I kept walking with my orb of light illuminating the area around us. But it was clear that Ana was in awe at the remains of the old war. No doubt wondering what had actually happened in the times of old.

Sighing loudly, I trekked on before she would start to ask the inevitable questions that I knew she was preparing in her mind. We walked towards the center of the cavern where an ominous violet light seemed to be seeping out of the stone floor. As we neared it began to glow brighter until I sent my orb of light towards it. It burst into a brilliant show of electrical tendrils and fire that circled and surrounded us. Images of my past battles danced in the fires as it showed my life.

I've seen this multiple times before. "Ana," I began as she watched one of my brothers get slain by a demon hoard. "These things happen," we watched as I tried to fight off my comrades to try and save Joe and Kekoa. The movements ended with Kekoa triggering a massive explosion that incinerated the hoard as a shield of holy light protected us.

"But... there was nothing you could do." She said now even more confused. Before it switched to our mission that I lost Jason.

"Jason tried to warn all of us, we didn't believe him." We watched as Jason drank the poison that ultimately ended his life. We watched as the crowd broke into chaos "as a leader I should have been the one to check the drinks..."

"But there was no way of knowing that it was poisoned. He died heroically" As she said that, we watched as the crowd turned on me and I told my team to leave as they belittled me. The parents of Jason screaming at me as they cradled his body. She couldn't hear what they were saying, but I was reliving these memories word for word...

"The best people you ever know, can and may fall in battle."

She watched as I lost Zoe and her brother. "How do you get over it."

I felt a tear fall from my watering eyes. I wiped them away before looking at her, "You don't. You just keep living for them. With their memories. Kailiana," I say as I hug her. "It's ok to cry." I say as she begins to weep again. "It's ok to be sad, but always live on, remember Axilious, remember Andreas. They are in your memories forever, and there is nothing wrong with that." I say holding her close. "I brought you here Ana, to show you that you don't have to be alone."

As I said this, the images change to that of all my friends. And my new family. "No one will be around forever, but we can make the most of every moment that we do have... together." The images ended on one of Ana, Bella, Nae, Steefas, everyone we care about. "Its with their help, that you will grow." I said before kissing her on the fore-head. "You deserved the truth 'Ana, and I know it's kind of late, but happy birthday."

We stayed there for while longer before I sprouted my wings again and flew us back to the others.

CHAPTER 26

Friends to Count On

The mood was somber when I returned with Kailiana. The loss of Andreas weighed heavily on all of us, yet there was little we could do. I kept hearing the persistent voice of the Lord telling me that we need to train, but after having such a massive blow to our emotional states, I knew we all needed a break and the Lord could sod off. Dehaas dropped in to inform me that from the original temporal displacement, time would now pass faster in this training area as pose to the modern world which would pass slower to us but normal time. One day now equated to that of a week. This was good as we were all able to recuperate and adjust to the new environment.

After approximately two weeks, I finally told Kailiana about what happened between me and Bella and just why I'd never truly forgive her. I'd accepted what happened in the past and her darkness as that doesn't define her anymore, but personally... that scar will always be there and never truly heal. I don't fault Kailiana for her faith in Bella because of what she has done for her. It's just a fact that the scars are too deep for myself... After this however, everything finally looked up was we all settled into a routine of hunt, sleep. Talk and then we started planning. Planning for the inevitable battles that were soon to be upon us. That's where we are now...

Sitting with the girls and Steefas, we all fell into a comfortable silence as our latest kill of some kind of massive lizard cooked over the fire. I wasn't that we'd never seen or eaten the critter before, its just that no one ever thought to name it. Thus it adopted the name of Lazard thing.

Thinking about our next move. We all looked into the crackling fire. Bella was the first to break the silence.

"We all need to continue training again, you know this Janix." I didn't say anything at first. Just lost in thought as I tried to think out a plan. I finally asked, "Where would we even begin, should I try to combine demon and angelic energy to complete what Lucifer tried to get me to do?"

"HELL NO!" Exclaimed Kailiana "You damn near killed yourself last time... no, there has to be another way."

I smiled at this, she really was too caring for her own good sometimes. "What do you suggest then? Honestly I'm all ears at this point."

"What if we're all looking at it wrong?" Asked Bel-la. "What if you're not supposed to control it?" I laughed at this.

"What am I supposed to do then? Let the energies and power consume me? We all saw what happened last time." I was truly at a loss for what she was suggesting.

"You tried to control the energy, you weren't letting your chakras align. It's the same principle as exuding holy light. Or even demonic power on its own. You don't control it... you just direct it." My hand was on my chin as I thought about it.

"You should listen to aunt Bella, daddy." Nae chirped in for the first time since the conversation began. I gave her a simple smile and a light nod as I thought about what I should try. It would go against everything I was taught and I would have to really let go and release the power that's been swirling inside trying so hard to escape.

"I see what you're saying..." With a heavy sigh, "it's easier said than done though..." and from what they already told me, the amount of power was.... unfathomable. Demonic energy is so unstable...

"Bella, what if… we contact RÿJunìc." Ana asked. Bella filtered her head.

"And why would we do that?"

"His sword!" I was trying to think of what they were getting at.

"What about his… that…" Bella stopped to ponder about what she was thinking. "Might actually work."

"What are y'all scheming about? What about RÿJunìc's sword." I asked even more confused than ever.

"Father," Ana started, "you know that your blade is only one half of a second right?" To which I nodded in affirmation. "Well RÿJunìc just so happens to wield the other half that belongs with your Shinxitar." It was then that all that they were talking about made sense.

"His blade, is Måkvalūr?" Contrary to my blade which loosely meant The Soulless Sword. Måkvalūr actually translated to Rising Valor. It was entertaining that the blade seems to have found just the right owner for itself as RÿJunìc was damn near the perfect warrior and knight. I thought about what they were implying and honestly, it just might work.

"Ana, contact our dear friend RÿJunìc. Its time we start taking the fight to Cûrburõs."

CHAPTER 27

A New Lesson

Another three days passed before we finally got word from RÿJunìc. The girls and Steefas were training. I was teaching Kailiana about her abilities to use magic just as her mother. She took to it like a natural, though, I had noticed that she was having a little difficulty with controlling her inner power. The power that allowed her create energy and manifest it into a single attack. I would have to figure out a way to calm Kailiana down so she could utilized this untaped power. As for her sword play, she was already a master assassin trained by the angels themselves. However, we have yet to officially spar. That will be a test for another time though.

Bella was teaching Nae how to defend herself from both magic and an attack from the blade. Much to her own ire, Nae was proving to be more like her father with very little affinity for the arcane arts. However she took to the bow like moth to a flame. Like her mother. Though slightly disappointing, its good to know what type of limitations she has, even at such a young age. This is vital when it comes down to properly training her. With or without magic. I'm figuring she will excel in defensive magic as it was nearly impossible to be born with no magic affinity considering who her mother is. But as for using it in combat, I can't see her developing the prowess for it.

Then there was Steefas, who was working on a new method of shadow warfare. He could solidify a shadow just enough that he could turn the edges into points and treat them as blades. He never knew that he could do that until we jokingly started messing with his powers to see what he could really do. Needless to say, everyone was shocked when I ended up with four tendrils of solidified shadow protruding from my arms and legs. Painful yes, but very educational. It was a discovery that we could never have thought possible had we not experimented. Never mind what he could possible do with his fire powers.

I'm going to make certain that I'm a fair distance way from the training area when this takes place.

I was leaning on a stone slab taking a breather after attempting to reshape the landscape again, I'd only been able to create half of what Lucifer had done when he first demonstrated what he could do. My dark matter lightning was all too weak, yet, it seemed as if my powers have reached a plateau. I had no idea how to breach this problem. Breathing heavy, I felt the presence of RÿJunìc finally manifest behind me.

Recomposing myself and with a heavy sigh, I turned to RÿJunìc. It took all of three seconds to comprehend that he was bleeding and riddled with arrows. He looked like a fluffy porcupine. Driving his blade into the stone in front of him, I just barely heard him with my enhanced hearing.

"He has risen." Before collapsing in his crimson armor.

"ANA! Bella!" I yelled for my daughter and fellow warrior. I didn't know what had happened but it was clear that we were out of time. Getting him up, we moved him to our sleeping area where we tended his wounds. It was clear from the damage on his armor that had he not been wearing it, he wouldn't be alive right now. The bite marks alone looked bad enough to cause him to bleed out and then there would have been no saving him. From the size of the markings, it was also clear that at some point he had been in the mouth of Cûrburõs. His unbreakable armor keeping him from being crushed. However his right arm was bent at an unnatural angel. Broken from the elbow.

140

Kailiana began working on him. Pushing as much healing magic into him as it was safe for her to do so. Yet even so, it was a slow process due to the extensive damage he'd taken. But there was still the question that worried all of us... how much time was really left... "Wake me up when you need to switch out. Then Bella and back. We will continue this until he wakes up and we have the answers that we've been looking for." I said to the group before calling Steefas over so we could relax before I had to take over the healing. Its definitely not my specialty, however even I can utilize at least the basic forms of healing curtesy of my Angelic Powers.

Laying down, I felt darkness envelope me. Enjoying a peaceful slumber, I was awoken to Kailiana informing me that it was my shift and that she needed some rest. Having gotten RÿJunìc out of immediate danger, all that was left was for the rest of us to keep healing him so that we kept our great ally alive and also our friend.

It was a calm few hrs. The crackling of the fire keeping us warm as the girls slept on Steefas soft fur coat. With a light greenish blue hue, my hands emitted light healing power. Nowhere near the scale of power that Ailani or Kailiana possessed but it was enough too lightly speed up the healing. Plus I was able to prolong it longer than the others as I had the extra endurance, even if it was only for the basic uses of healing. If it was worse, then I'd still be utterly useless. My talent for the darker side of magic, I regretfully say is far more superior. Great for combat and the arcane magic but not so much when it comes to light magic and my angelic powers are really the only reason that I'm even able to use healing magic at all.

RÿJunìc began to stir a little in his slumber, in apparent discomfort and had a pained expression evident as he seemed to be reliving whatever hell he went through be-fore coming to us. His body scared to hell from his intensive training that he had undergone as a servant of that pit. The amount of missions that he had no doubt been on for the sake of Lucifer himself was evident as the marks left him many reminders. The trial he must have undergone. Honestly, I couldn't help but think about what would happen if we were to properly fight.

"Don't think I'm out of commission just yet Lord Janix, it'll take a hell of a lot more than some mangey mut to eradicate the likes of the Knights of Hell and their commander." He's said proudly as I couldn't help but chuckle at his brashness. Even when it seemed that he wouldn't make it he was still gonna show off the might of a Commander.

"Wouldn't dream of writing you off mate. But you still need to heal and though I may not be the best on for the job, I'm pushing everything I can to help you." He simply chuckled before sitting up and shakily forcing himself too stand. "You shouldn't do that yet!!!!!"

"Never mind that Lord Janix, we have work to do and very little time. HE has risen." RÿJunìc stood even if shakily, drawing his blade. "I was informed that this is what you were seeking and what you need in order to fight the evil that's come to our world. I don't know how this will be able to help," He whipped it out before offering me the hilt. Taking it gingerly, I looked at him before feeling an incredible power pulse through me. Like when I was first flying over the city, it felt as if my very being was being ripped apart and cast into the realm of darkness. It was clear that whatever with-in this blade… it's not only a sword of anti-matter. But it felt like it was rejecting me. My hand began to burn as the hilt turned red hot. Dropping the blade I clutched my hand before looking at the faint purplish glow that was around the blade itself.

Runes slowly began to appear along the edge of the black blade. Yellow lighting danced on the blade before the tip began to glow with power.

BANG!!!!

I was thrown back by a massive blast that shook the environment around us, the wind knocked out of me. My limbs aching as I sat there just thinking. I heard someone kneel next to me without saying anything.

"Well that fucking sucked." I said to RÿJunìc who just laughed with mirth.

"To understand my blade Lord Janix, you must first allow the anger and hate to dissipate. Contrary to what your blade is like, this one is fueled and controlled by emotion. Yours is vast like the galaxies in which the Lord himself created. Yet my blade, is as ever flowing like the ethereal energy of the divine." RÿJunìc informed me while helping me up off the ground. Picking up his blade, he held it out to me. "Try again why don't you?"

With a deep sigh, I couldn't help but grimace before steeling my nerves. Now was not the time to doubt myself. Now was not the time to give up I must learn to utilize this blade if I ever plan to have a chance at defeating Cûrburõs.

CHAPTER 28

Simple Understanding

'*Release the hate within me...*' I thought... easier said than done.

I let my scarred fingers clasp the hilt of the blade and suddenly felt, ease. For all of five seconds nothing happened. Until I noticed that I was no longer in the same place I once was. There was this haze around the every-thing, it was hot. I felt the heat of what I now saw as fire...

Fire that danced all around me. The air dry and heat scorching. The flames that danced around me formed a swirling circular vortex that swirled upward until it formed a dome above me. Within the fire though, I was seeing flashes of instances that have already passed. Instances that were happening right now as Cûrburõs razed a city that he was in right now. It looked to be one of the north eastern Provences. But then... the images shifted to that of my friends and family, fighting for their lives as the minions of Cûrburõs swarmed us from all sides. We were surrounded, and loosing badly. The lycans, fighting as best they could but even with their healing properties, they weren't immune to total dismemberment. The people of Véchenti fighting but falling all the same. They stood no match against the demons that fought with Cûrburõs. The children of Steefas, also fighting valiantly but falling all the same. We were done for... we were on our last legs. I was seeing the demise of humanity. In all our glory. I felt hope leaving me... I felt as hope was abandoned.

That is until I saw her. My gut clenched when she stood, bloodied from her own injuries and of fallen foes. My daughters together, stood atop a mound of dead demons while chanting, little Nae who was now at least thirteen fighting and holding the demons back as power surged through her sister. This spell that she's about to cast, will save us all, that is... if she had ever been able to cast it. I watched as Cûrburõs massive jaws came down, taking Kailiana's head in one bit. Nae frozen as she saw the death of her sister before a demon spear pierced her side, the tail of Cûrburõs swept across her. Time seemed to freeze in her gaze, as I watched myself finally show up cutting down demons before my eyes landed on Nae who fell after being split in half and her headless sister. I watched as Ailani was overwhelmed with demons before she was dismembered by each limb. I watched as Steefas himself swallowed a little demon before bursting into gore as the demon exploded from within him. We had lost... and there was nothing more that we could do... then with a bright flash of purplish light, it dispersed in all directions. Once again I was in a different area.

I felt liquid falling down my bare chest, my right face hot and damp with sweat and... blood I realized. It seemed that I was beyond injured and blood poured down my body as I was on my knees. Måkvalūr broken and bent in directions a sword never should be. The power flickering as the blade itself lost it's mystical properties... I myself was alone... The silence killing me... they were all just alive a moment ago... my family, my friends... all of them gone in an instant... because I was too late. It's always this way. Just when something good happens... I lose the ones I love... I lose the things that make it worth it. WHATS THE DAMN POINT IN EVEN LIVING!!!!

With a head held high, I screamed. Into the night. I screamed. Into the eyes of Cûrburõs himself I screamed as I collapsed. I was done. They were all gone. Cûrburõs can have this fucking world for all I care. There's no point to me fighting anymore. There's no point to me trying to survive anymore. I just want the pain to stop. The ringing... the voices of loved ones, the faces that keep flashing before my eyes. I want it all to stop...I was beyond myself as tears streamed down my eyes. As I looked at Cûrburõs in a pleading way to just end it all right now. To take this pain away. He's taken everything and everyone. The few he didn't left anyway so why should I keep living. With his tail raised he flicked it towards me, something landed by my broken blade Måkvalūr. Without think, I raised Shinxitar above my head. Blade pointed for my abdomen. All I saw was red through my tears of anger, pain, sadness. All the emotions that were clashing together...

It was then that I was jolted awake, using my attachment to Shinxitar to pull my blade to my hand rearming myself. My body steaming, the heat still present and the emotions very real. That wasn't just a dream... that wasn't just a vision... that was... that was a promised future. One that we can't... one that won't be changed.

"Father!!!" Yelped Kailiana, who dropped the contents she was holding before enveloping me in a tight hug. She moved so fast that even my reflexes didn't have time to comprehend that she had just rushed me while I had Shinxitar drawn. It took me a few moments to fully relax and comprehend just what was happening right now. Yet when I did I dropped my weapon and returned the hug. Taking solace that she was in fact, still alive... for now.

"We were all so worried... well, mostly everyone." She said with relief before adopting a wistful expression. Withdrawing from the embrace I gave her a strange look before I heard a throat being cleared behind her.

"Well look who finally decided to wake up." Came the condescending voice of Ailani. My face fell, of all people... why her and why now. For all my intelligence, when my gaze met hers, all I could really muster was "Sup Ailani."

The silence that followed was painful. Time stopped and the three of us just stood there with our gazes on each other. Kailiana more awkward than myself and her mother. To be fair, the last time she saw us was Ailani attempting to take my head off. I was about to trail off into more personal thoughts until Ailani spoke up.

"You really haven't changed." She scoffed, but before leaving I couldn't help but notice how her gaze seemed to, for the fraction of a second, soften and real worry flash in her eyes. But then as quick as the look showed it was hidden by a look of scorn again. Anna and I shared a strange expression before laughing.

"Sup Ailani?" Anna gasped. "Are you serious?!??" She was laughing ridiculously and I wasn't any better.

"It was the best that I could muster after such an awkward wake up." I replied with a very sheepish look.

She rolled her eyes before looking at me. "Only you could come up with such an incredibly stupid response after being in a coma for three days."

"Three again???"

"Yeah, I don't know what you saw, RÿJunìc told us that the second time you attempted to work with the weapons… you just collapsed." It was beyond reason, the vision I saw suddenly coming back to my memory. I couldn't help but wonder what it was that it was supposed to mean and whether or not I could actually help with any-thing that was remotely part of the tasks at hand. In the end though I can't help that if something didn't change and fast, that I would have to see it become a reality.

...

No… that's not even an option. That isn't even an idea. That will not… it cannot happen. I won't let it happen. No matter what, no one will die… I will not lose any-more friends or family. I have to become stronger. I will become stronger.

"Master!?!!" Came the inquiring voice of Steefas.

"What's up Steefas?" I asked curious to his strange tone of voice.

'*Well, you have to see it to believe it.*'

'*Alright, Kailiana and I will be out in a sec.*' I men-tally told Steefas before verbally speaking to Ana.

"Looks like there is something strange outside. Time to see what's up I guess." I said to Kailiana.

Walking outside, I couldn't help but see that there was a massive looking stallion outside the tent with beautiful ice blue eyes that seemed to piece into your soul. I noticed how it seemed that the main was swirling and… glowing. It was white and sparkling as if moonlight were reflecting off of it. Well, reflecting wouldn't really be the right word. I suppose emitting would be better suited for what was really happening. A number of emotions swirled through my mind while gazing upon the stallion. Everyone seemed to be entranced, Bella appeared to almost be trans-fixed with her gaze on him, but what I didn't realize is that the stallion also had its eyes locked onto Bella.

Time was all but frozen, as if nothing even mat-tered. Everyone locked in a trance. That is until the massive horse took a step forward toward Bella effectively breaking Steefas out of his own stupor faster than the rest of us.

He released a mighty growl when before charging at the stallion before launching himself. However, before Steefas massive jaws could clamp down on the stallions neck, it began to glow brighter before emitting an energy shock wave sending all of us to our knees. The Stallion snorted before walking up to Bella and sniffing her hair. Bella herself just sitting, still as a statue looking into the stallions eyes.

CHAPTER 29

New Partner's

Bella's POV

For what seemed like an eternity, it seemed as if I was frozen, lost in the gaze of the Stallion. But... at the same time I didn't just see the Stallion, I saw every stupid thing I've done, I saw every horrible thing that Lord Lucifer ordered me to do as I helped in the building of his empire from the ground up. The legions of demons I've personally led against the beings known as mankind... the shit that I've done to ensure demonic rebellions were snuffed out so Lucifer didn't have to soil his hands. Even if he was more than willing to for the sake of keeping order in Hell. It didn't matter, He was my lord and for some reason, all the things that never bothered me before suddenly came to light as this bloody stallion peered into my soul.

What everyone seems to forget however, is that I didn't start off as a roving angel, hell, I didn't even start as a demon, I was a pitiful mortal that was just looking for her place in the lords world. Born just a few years after the great fall of eden, my father being Cain himself.

'But you'd never hear about that, all you readers care about is that little shit Abel. He wasn't even that special.'

Anyway, I'm getting off topic, I lived just as long as all the other men, yet I was written out of the books Bella being a name I gave myself once my lord saved me. My real name being Adira slave to Alkäinin. By all accounts, I never deserved the accomplishments that Lucifer gave me the opportunity to obtain. I was a slave, violated and dis-graced yet... he saved me. Where I came from didn't matter to him... and... When Lord Lucifer first took me in from the little village that was wiped out by God himself. I realized that I finally had purpose. These all came out as the stallion judged me, and not even Janix could save me this time. Even if I wanted to help myself, I quickly realized that I couldn't move, there was an ethereal field around us. Literally freezing everything in time.

"*Well?*" I heard a voice that sounded strong and deep from nowhere... that finally broke me out of my stagnant state. Looking around to see who said something but Janix and everyone else appeared to be frozen in time while I was able to move. Confused now, I turned to look behind me, "Me you dunce!" I froze again, before looking directly back at the horse. I couldn't help but think about the time that Nix told me about his meeting with Steefas.

"Are... are you the one that spoke?" I asked to the horse.

"*And she finally figures it out, damn you're a slow one aren't you.*" The horse replied while I continued to sit there and wait. "*Please don't tell me that I found my partner only to discover that she's a half pint?*"

"What are...? Who are you?" More and more questions just seemed to keep rattling in my mind before it finally hit me. "You're the son of Hayagriva aren't you, Lümffemm"

"Exactly and as much as I hate the idea as you would never comprehend the might and power of the great Hayagriva; but in these trying times, even I must have a companion."

"But... why come here? And why talk to me???"

"You damn dunce!!! Did I not just say that you're the one I'm supposed to partner with." Lümffemm replied. Stomping his hove dramatically.

I replied with something intelligent like "...Oh."

"I don't like the idea any more than you do, but to survive we've gotta make a lot of choices and sacrifices, some of us more than others." It still didn't make any sense to me but in the end what part of any of this made sense in regards to our little band of fighters. "Also your friends are about to come out of their moment of frozen time, do not let them attack me or I will be harsher then I already was with that damn puppy." I had seconds to comprehend what he said before, "BELLA!!!" Janix exclaimed.

"I'm fine Nix! Don't worry, he's not going to hurt us." Standing up before giving Lümffemm a simple nod of acknowledgement and standing in the way of a very enraged Steefas. "Lümffemm here has come to, to…" I stop, realizing that I have little to no idea how to explain the situation to the group.

"I am here to become Bella's partner. Also to lend my assistance in your little war with the Hell bringer Cûburõs." Lümffemm summarized…

Janix POV

I don't know what the hell just happened, however it comes down to there had to have been a time shift. For one second we see the large stallion approaching us, but then I see Bella getting in the way of us from attacking. As all I could think is that she's about to be lost… Once again I'm about to lose another that I couldn't protect, some one that was putting their faith in me and I couldn't save them once again. It was in this moment that I realized that I had grown to… damn it all that I had grown to appreciate her as a friend. Someone who could possibly lead me out of the darkness. Someone who could lead me back to the light and fill that hole in my heart that was left twice before, but can I really accept that????

I… I don't know, in the end it will all be the same. There's nothing I can do… the lord himself manipulated me twice before, it will just happen again while I try to do the right thing I will just lose another and then the cycle will start all over again, and this time I will probably not come out of the stupor. This time, I may just say screw the world and let Cûburõs win. Two massive wars…TWO. And I almost lost two children during them. One of which I never even knew until most recently.

This doesn't mean anything, but it doesn't matter. I need to watch over little Nae. Hell, Ailani is now acknowledging me again, but what good is that when I don't have the means of getting her to understand everything that happened. She was locked in her own mind for over a year and then suddenly thrust back into the fray… No, I can under-stand her anger. It's exactly how I almost was when I was first introduced to my daughter, my first daughter who hated me. I…meeting her was like a sword to the gut… or even like one of the dwarfs flint lock pistols that they are still in testing.

I'm no better, as I slaughtered an entire village just because of the death of my cousin… Kailiana's only father figure that truly knew her. Sighing, I stood up thinking about the things that have been happening over the last few days until finally, "Who are you and why are you here?" I inquired of the horse.

"I am the lord of horses, I am the father of Stallions, I am Lümffemm, The Midnight light." The beautiful yet dangerous Stallion now known as Lümffemm replied proudly.

"I think I like that," Bella commented. It made sense, that she would be drawn to the stallion that just radiates power. "It matches your ethereal glow and the power of the sea that seems to be radiating. I shall call you that. My friend."

For all of a moment I thought that the horse was going to trample her yet all he did was walk up and nudge her with his head"

"No one has ever called me by my other name, but I think I will allow it this time, as you're my chosen partner. I will be with you faithfully."

Steefas released a massive growl before nodding his head in a simple *begrudging* form of acceptance.

Although it was nice that we now had another ally, I couldn't help but think about the way Midnight is showing up all of a sudden.

Midnight you said you came here to join us, but what is it that your here for." I asked simply thinking that there is no way that this is just a coincidence.

"You are correct leader of the 7th legion. Cûrburõs is taking over more and more of the free world and there is little to no existence." Midnight neighed loudly.

I haven't been called that in a long time I thought as the environment once again shook and everything seemed to shimmer, as iff the whole training area was falling and we seemed to be shifting back to the natural plain of existence. I saw trees and a very red and dark sky. But then shades and shades of shadows flickered into existence.

"Whats happening!" cried little Nae. Bell and I looked at each other before brandishing our weapons. Cry's of hell seemed to be manifesting, fire engulfing the land-scape. There was light and darkness all swirling together as a massive hell hound suddenly launched at me from a shade in the trees only to be subdued by Steefas.

What the hell is wrong with you?" Growled a very displeased Steefas who had his hackles raised and ready to deliver the final blow. That said, the enemy hound rolled from under him tripping Steefas up before its massive jaw clamped down on Steefas shoulder causing the soul of agony to be heard. Shadows began to swirl as I watch multiple of Steefas children manifest from the shadows and stand around him. Some of them pointing outwards as they were making sure that we were staying away. The message was clear, no interference would be tolerated.

CHAPTER 30

Truths Behind the Anger

We were all looking on as Steefas dealt with this hell hound. Having no idea to what was going on aside from one of Steefas offspring going rogue, nor could we even help because of the nature of this fight. The attack was direct and an indication in the ways of the hell hounds as a challenge against the leader. Whoever came out on top would be the Alpha and nothing would stop this.

"Child of shadows and darkness what's become of you?" Steefas tried as the hound attempted to bite Steefas only slashed in the face and rammed which sent the hound through the air and landing in a heap. "Do you not recognize your king and father?" We could only watch as Steefas tried in vain to get his former subordinate under control but it was as if the Hell hound was sick. It was then that I noticed something odd, not only was the hound not reacting to what Steefas was saying, but it seemed that there seemed to be some sort of foam at the corners of the this rogues mouth.

'Steefas, do you see the foam?'

'Kind of hard to miss mast...' he was interrupted from replying to me as the hound tried in vain to start swiping at Steefas. Attempting to bite off Steefas tail.

'This damn mut!' Steefas growled to me as he realized what almost happened.

"Last chance, though I normally respect a grab for power, you are clearly out of your league." Steefas stated with power before letting a hint of his true power out. His entire form seemed to flicker as he suddenly looked more shadow than wolf. I could only watch as tendrils of shadow wrapped around the hound before another more solid shadow took the hounds head.

Just like that, the fight was over, it was almost too fast to believe... and too simple, I nodded to the other hell hounds who were acting as security before I walked to Steefas.

"You ok?" I asked him. Putting a hand on his before looking at his wound.

"Steefas, will you let me help?" Came the voice of the woman I didn't think would have come to us.

"Ailani?" I asked to which she cast a short gaze over me.

"I'm offering to because it is my duty as a *healer*. Although you're the one who trained me to be both a healer and an Assassin remember." Ailani asked in a very simple yet monotone voice.

"That..." Steefas grunted, "Would be much appreci-ated Lady Ailani." Steefas gave me a look that conveyed the message, he would be fine and he wanted to have a private moment with Ailani.

Ailani Pov.

That idiot... sometimes I have to wonder why the hell he has to be so damn dense. "Not gonna stay and watch over your friend?" I asked.

"I have faith in both of you Ailani, I'm sure that you have more than enough skills to heal my best friend." Janix said before turning his back to me. Once out of eye sight I couldn't help but sigh... same dense idiot that I love. Walking over to Steefas I began healing his wound slowly allowing it to close so that we had a moment to speak. Once Nix was out of ear shot though, "It's been a long time Steefas. I hope you've been taking better care of yourself then he was." I listened as I heard him sigh before responding.

"Indeed it has Lani, though I wish that you would end this little charade. Surely you know that he still loves you and will never be the same without you by his side. You were and still are his everything, his reason to live. Hell, I don't need to tell you the amount of panic attacks that he had when he left you with Alex..." I couldn't help but flick his oddly adorable wolf ear.

"You both left me with him. Though I won't deny that the peace was nice, you both left me with holes and longing..." I could feel the tear welling up in my eyes but I steeled my nerves. I lightly pat Steefas ear that I flicked as a small apology.

"But I do see what you mean... I just thought that he would have at least tried to approach me by now about... well... anything." I was honestly exasperated at this point. He's seen how strong I was, even when I acted like I discarded his training and took up the armor that he told me to get rid of so long ago. I thought it would be a nice little bit of fun for us to break the ice again as warriors... but then fucking Andreas had to knock me out as I was going to surprise Janix with a kiss. I'm absolutely pissed at him... but I love him. With all my heart still. It hurts to see him surrounded by so many beautiful women...

"Lani, he's once again juggling the world on his shoulders though it may have worked any other time and been cute to you two, everyone is on edge." I could only sigh, he was right of course... but it wasn't like we wouldn't pull though, especially with the Knights of Hell and someone like Kailiana on our side.

"Steefas, who are those other girls?" I could only snicker as Steefas cocked his wolf head to the side as if asking what I meant.

"That girl... the one thats always around him... what kind of relationship do they have." Steefas tensed at that. I didn't like that...

"Lady Ailani..." he tried to begin before I interjected.

"Don't you bullshit me Steefas. I can make this healing a lot more painful if you like." I knew in that moment my eyes flashed silver. I had been training with he mages of Anubis but keeping full control at all times was difficult.

"Lani, I can promise you that they are nothing more than good friends. Beyond that is not my place to say, as that is their business and not my word to share."

"Oh really" I said with quite a bit of irritation, but I understood. This was Janix best friend after all. "Well, in any case I need to get a moment with him without anyone interrupting." I still didn't like the way that he tensed. "Well, its about time that I leave y'all for the moment then, I have other tasks to accomplish before the end of everything." I said getting up.

"He needs you. Y'all have a lot to talk about and before the day is over y'all really should talk about the other two. And… about another few details." Steefas told me cryptically before vanishing in shadow.

As much as I wanted to just run to Janix, I had other tasks to take care of and I need to get in contact with Cain. He will be needed and finally get rid of his little excuse that he's "lost" limbs. With this war on the horizon, it was clear that even he would need to pull his ancient weapon from the ground once more.

Drawing my blade, I cut a hole into space and time creating a portal. Neat little trick that I stole from Dehaas after he brought me from whatever white room we were at. The same room that I got all my memories back. Stepping though I found myself in the village of Véchenti. Now being fortified and turned into the headquarters of the united army. Similar to that of assault on Michaels Headquarters, we would use the Lycans as the front troops who would take the brunt of the attacks before allowing our archers to get proper ranges. The mages who were on the march from the Northern province where they would once again join us in battle against the forces of evil. After the battle with Michael, the mages all but disappeared from the surrounding area. It was then that I learned after reviewing texts in the Temple of Adonai, discovering the existence of an entire kingdom full of mages. Turns out the large faction that assisted us just happened to be around our province spreading their teachings. Which just happens to be where Albright was from. Having gone AWOL to join Smee, becoming a magical merchant.

"Lani?" Came the voice of Aarönin. My face lit up upon seeing the older man. He was always kind to myself and Janix.

"Aarönin! It's so good to see you." I said before hugging him tightly.

"Ailani, I didn't think that I'd ever see you in that armor again." Being honest if I didn't need to be in this battle, I probably wouldn't have gotten in this battle armor again either, as my love wouldn't have let me remember. Just the thought of what he did made my blood boil. I'm not sure if I'll ever get over it completely. I'll acknowledge that what he did was for me but I can still be sour about it. Not to mention the fact that he's always around those two other women. I don't know why I seem to have this distain for Bella or Kailiana but it's just this prevalent feeling. That said… I also can't shack this feeling that I know her from somewhere… same with little Nae… I definitely need more answers before the end of the day.

"Honestly neither did I… after having my damn memories taken the way they were." Aarönin frowned be-fore saying "None of use wanted to hide that portion of your life from you, you can't imagine how hard it was to teach… my children not to say anything." Tears filled his eyes as he was brought back to those horrible memories. My eyes also began to water before pulling him into another hug.

"I'm so sorry that this happened…" "Never mind that right now." He cut me off pulling away. "We have much to discuss,

Cain is in Janix's bunker. As of now we've gotten majority of the allies into it aside from a select few that need to be up top and Steefas children have been doing their best to watch over us. Security is a lot easier to keep up with them around. Forgive me but I have a few other tasks to discuss with Hägrīs." Aarönin relayed to me before walking away to speak with the King of the Lycans.

Nodding, I also walked to my old home, I was able to find his home without any problems. The home that we use to share. The home that we finally confessed our love. My heart broke a little upon seeing the state of it. The once clean and tight knit room was now compiled full of crates and boxes. It was clear that it hasn't had an actual occupant for a while from the amount of dust on the crates. There was very little that I could see that seemed to actually belong to Nix. "What happened to you my love..." I whispered before walking up to a bookshelf that was untouched. Pulling halfway out a very red looking book, it unlocked a few mechanisms before the entire shelf opened up.

Just like you Nix. Always one for the theatrical stealth devises.

A long stairwell opened up to me letting me through before the book shelf closed itself again. Bioluminescent mushrooms lit up the stairway allowing me to see where I was going as I walked down a good hundred steps before coming upon a hallway which branched into three other directions. Picking the one going left for a few meters, I exited the hallway into a large hall that looked to be the main dining facility. There were many people here just relaxing and talking. I noticed in some corners that there seemed to be uniformed guards with extravagant looking armor and golden Sabers. Then another door at the end of the hall. Considering that it was give or take noon, *I really need to get myself one of those time pieces that most of leadership have*, I will assume that Cain would be enjoying his own lunch. So I walked through to one of the guards who as soon as he noticed me locked his body and gave me a salute.

"Good morning Ma'am. I was not expecting a General to be visiting us this afternoon." Confused I saluted back before asking, "Good morning soldier, but how do you know that I'm a General?" To which he looked at me with a very strange look of disbelief.

"Ma'am, with all due respect, how could anyone not know the former mate to High Commander Janix?" He explained like it was common knowledge.

"I see," I started to take notice that there was really no noise and turning around I saw that the entire room had gone silent upon realizing who I was. It was then that one of the guards yelled out **"GRÃTUS CHI ALSKEP AVE KENAROL AILANI!"** Or very loosely translated *"EVERYONE THANKS YOU GENERAL AILANI!"* Everyone in the area stopped what they were doing, the men and women with food putting their chow down before joining the room in rendering a salute.

"Ma'am I know you probably don't remember most of us. But you've saved just about everyone in this room at least once. It is an honor to be in your presence." He said before giving me a salute. I was so taken aback that for a moment I couldn't do anything but look around. It was then that I noticed that I have indeed seen most if not all of these faces at one point or another. Lycans, men, women, djinn, and many others. I have healed this entire room for one thing or another. Saluting back I couldn't help but feel an odd sensation that ran though me during the recognition.

"I remember all of you. Sgt. Kĩjuine." I said before asking both the guard who I now recognized as Jakeb. A newer soldier that joined the legion about a year ago. Impressive that he was able to become one of Janix personal guardsmen. "Have either of you seen Cain?"

"Yes ma'am. He's just left the hall down to the lower levels. I believe he went back to his quarters. Would you like me to escort you?" Sgt. Kĩjuine asked politely.

"Please do." We left the dining hall and made our way downstairs and though the maze of tunnels that were illuminated by more bioluminescent mushrooms. Janix really did do a lot of work putting this place together just to keep everyone safe. Before long we ended up at another room that held five doors with names on them. Janix, Ailani, Alex, Cain and Flores, I found it interesting that my room was next to Janix until Sgt. Kĩjuine explained that despite what commander Janix wanted, Alex in secret made sure that my room was in-between the two of them. I could only nod my head before thanking Sgt. Kĩjuine. Knocking on the door with Cain's name, it wasn't Cain that opened the door. What I was before me caused my hair to stand on end. Primal fear enveloped me as I gazed upon what was in front of me. A very large fox with red and yellow streaks passing through its fur. Emerald eyes that screamed intelligence while also piercing into my very soul. He looked strong and proper. Yet also deadlier than anything I've ever encountered. The amount of ancient power rolling over me from this fox made me feel small and insignificant. It was then he finally spoke.

"So she finally has her memories back." Came a soothing voice from the fox. **"Its good timing too as hope was all but abandoned…"**

EPILOGUE

In a timeless void

The divine being continued to observe through liquid mercury as the girl told the story. The atrium was quite, as they listened to the story. It was late into the night now as I recounted the tales of my family. The disaster that happened when my mother got her memories back. And the havoc that was left behind. *"This is just what happened a few days before Cûrburōs showed up. A few days before he destroyed everything that we all knew. A few days before my father abandoned us... the last few days before hope was abandoned."*

CHARACTER ART

Janix— veteran hero. Blood of both Arch angel and Demon. Chosen replacement of God

Steefas— Best friend to Janix. Father of hell hounds, Lord of Fire and Shadow.

Cûrburōs also known as Tiléqan, Victēncy, Anubisety.